Whistling in the Dark

Other Books by George Garrett

Short Fiction
King of the Mountain
In the Briar Patch
Cold Ground Was My Bed Last Night
A Wreath for Garibaldi
The Magic Striptease
An Evening Performance

Novels
The Finished Man
Which Ones Are the Enemy?
Do, Lord, Remember Me
Death of the Fox
The Succession
Poison Pen
Entered from the Sun

Poetry
The Reverend Ghost
The Sleeping Gypsy
Abraham's Knife
For a Bitter Season
Welcome to the Medicine Show
Luck's Shining Child
The Collected Poems of George Garrett

Plays
Sir Slob and the Princess
Enchanted Ground

Biography
James Jones

Criticism
Understanding Mary Lee Settle
The Sorrows of Fat City

Whistling in the Dark

TRUE STORIES AND OTHER FABLES

George Garrett

Harcourt Brace Jovanovich, Publishers

New York   San Diego   London

HBJ

Requests for permission to make copies of any
part of the work should be mailed to:
Copyrights and Permissions Department,
Harcourt Brace Jovanovich, Publishers, 8th Floor,
Orlando, Florida 32887.

Library of Congress Cataloging-in-Publication Data
Garrett, George P., 1929–
Whistling in the dark: true stories and other fables/George
Garrett.—1st ed.
p.   cm.
ISBN 0-15-191313-7
I. Title.
PS3557.A72W55   1992
813'.54—dc20   91-45012

Designed by Lydia D'moch

Printed in the United States of America

First edition
A B C D E

For Jane Gelfman

What can I do but babble this nonsense and report prodigies which no one else will believe, except I believe in you always as I believe my own name.

—"Apology"

The spirit
moves within memory, and only there. . . .
            —*Julia Randall,* "Moving in Memory"

I desire that all men should see me in my
simple, natural, and ordinary fashion, without straining or artifice; for it is myself that
I portray.
    —*The Essays of Michel Eyquem de Montaigne*

If you need to remember anything,
It is the best way home.
            —*R.H.W. Dillard,* "Gettysburg"

Contents

Whistling in the Dark

Whistling
in the Dark

1.

Two men dressing. They are wearing GI undershorts and shiny dog tags like necklaces. They are freshly shaved and showered. Their hair is cut short on top and sidewalled. They are flat-stomached and hard-muscled. Two American soldiers in a large high-ceilinged room located in the heart of an old Luftwaffe barracks a little to the south of the city of Linz. It's a fine stone, permanent barracks, the best these two soldiers have lived or will live in. Waxed and shiny hardwood floors, high clear windows overlooking a grassy parade ground. In this room there are maybe half a dozen cots, neat and tight, perfectly made up, shiny green footlockers with names and serial numbers painted on the lids of each. There are large, ample wooden wall lockers that the Krauts left behind, left open now with GI uniforms, khaki at this season, the ODs recently packed away, hanging perfectly in strict proscribed rows.

The two soldiers are carefully and awkwardly dressing,

their twin cigarettes casting shimmying veils of pale smoke from a butt can. Awkwardly because they do not wish to sit on and muss up their beds while dressing. If they sit, to lace up boots for example, they will have to use a footlocker for a chair. Their khakis are tailored snug and crisp from starched ironing, creases as straight and keen as a razor's edge. Their brass, collar brass and belt buckles, glitters. They have put their buckles on backward to save them from scratches, for the soldiers will be wearing pistol belts, too. Their cordovan-dyed jump boots are spit-shined and glossy. They have put in white laces and will be wearing white gloves, too, and white chin straps on their simonized helmet liners. Red artillery scarves instead of neckties. The blue-and-white TRUST patches, worn on the left shoulders and proudly set off with flashy white cross-stitching, that show they come from the old 351st Regimental Combat Team in Trieste, have now been removed and replaced by some bland patch or other. (Whose shape and color and meaning I have long since forgotten.) Indicating that they are serving in Austria. But anyone with a trained eye and any interest would know right away that they come from somewhere else. Most likely TRUST, but maybe from the 6th Infantry in Berlin, which affects some of the same singular style: dyed black-web equipment; pistol belts (in this case, with each and every one of their tiny brass eye-lets buffed to remove the paint and grit to the metal and give it a high, bright shine, confirmed with clear nail polish); first-aid pouches hung on the left hip; and ammo pouches, holding two full clips of forty-five-caliber cartridges, worn up front just to the right—two eyelets over, I seem to recall—of the belt buckle. On the right hip they hang gleaming dark leather holsters holding the .45 pistols that they have been issued for today. Last of all, each puts on a brass whistle on a chain,

attached to the left shirt-pocket button, and an arm band—
MP for Military Police. There is no MP unit up here near
Linz. Which, except for the Four Power City of Vienna, deep
in the Russian Zone, is as far forward as Americans are. Just
across the river, the dirty old Danube, from the Russkies.
There are said to be about forty thousand of them over there.
Over here we have a reconnaissance battalion, an old outfit
that has been here a good while, an infantry battalion, and
ourselves, the 12th Field Artillery Battery (Separate). In the-
ory we have come here in response to the fact that they have
suddenly, and for no discernible reason, moved those forty
thousand combat troops into advance positions on the other
side of the river. Should they decide to come across, to attack,
that is, it is our function in this post to try to delay them for
a period of between fifteen minutes and half an hour. That
will give the main body of American forces in Salzburg, and
farther west in Germany, time enough to take their defensive
positions.

These two men have drawn MP duty on a quiet Saturday
in springtime. Fully dressed and ready, they will be briskly
inspected by somebody or other, the officer of the day most
likely, or maybe the sergeant of the guard; then they will pick
up a Jeep at the motor pool and drive into the city.

It is a clear bright day. And now these two, coming outside from the barracks, are jointly astonished to see a ring of
distant snow-capped mountains all around. It has been so gray
and close, wet and foggy since they got here that they never
knew there were mountains within sight until this minute.
They don't say anything. What is there to say? They are old-
timers, short timers in the U.S. Army now. It is not that they
are not surprised. It is that they are continually astonished by
everything. They don't speak, but they stop in midstride. They

stand there and just look around. The young corporal allows himself to whistle softly between his teeth.

"Let's go," the sergeant says then. "We're fixing to be late."

They move off side by side, in step. I can't remember the corporal's name for the life of me. The sergeant, of course, is myself.

2.

They pass by the gate guards and turn left on the highway heading for Linz. You can be sure that, without a word, a glance, or a nudge, they are both smiling for at least a moment. They sit in the front seats of the Jeep, the corporal driving, very straight, both of them feeling almost fragile as they seek to keep every crease and part of their uniforms crisply unwrinkled. They want to be sharp-looking downtown. They like to show the local girls, whores and shack-jobs, and hamburger bandits that Americans in uniform can look every bit as sharp as (everybody says) the Krauts did. Going out of the gate and turning left and north, they both smile into the breeze.

They are thinking about the moment they first arrived at that same gate maybe a month or so ago. How they left Trieste secretly by night. Went first to a staging area in pine woods near Pisa. Rumor was they were going to Greece, somewhere like that. Who knew? Anyway, they painted over all the unit numbers on all the vehicles. Got rid of patches and anything identifying them as coming from Trieste. They were loaded on trucks with all the canvas laced tight and sent off in small convoys, a few at a time, up north through the high Brenner Pass and into Austria. Nobody, except ranking officers, knew where they were headed until they actually got there. Except, of course (as ever and always), somebody goofed. Somebody forgot or maybe never knew that the vehicles of the Austrian command, alone of all commands in the U.S. Army, did not use a large white star, on each side of the vehicle and on top of the hood, as an identifying marker. For all our care and secrecy we were known at once, at first sight, as convoys coming from elsewhere by our gleaming white stars. Every spy between Pisa and Linz would have noted our coming and going. So that when we arrived at the old Luft-waffe camp and some guy in the outfit turned on his battery-powered portable radio, we picked up, from the Russian side, in good English, "Greetings to the men of the Twelfth Field Artillery on their safe arrival at Linz."

But that is not worth the kind of smile the two GIs are smiling. What has them grinning is the subject of women. When we pulled out of Trieste suddenly, the group had to say good-bye to their girlfriends (and semipermanent shack-jobs). Some of these couples had been together for years. Some of them had children, illegitimate, of course, because it was an extremely difficult and complex process for a GI to marry a Triestene woman. It was not encouraged. Nevertheless, leaving was a wrench for all of them. A time of tears and gloom. Promises to write. Promises to meet again, somehow, someday. The gloom lasted for a few days over in the tent camp near Pisa, until it gradually began to dawn on all the guys that wherever they went next—to Greece or North Africa or the freaking South Pole—they would be starting over. A new deal. All-new girls. So by the time we were loaded, that was all the guys (especially the bona fide, certified lover boys) could think and talk about—the new and improved stuff, *strange nookie!* they were going to be enjoying very soon.

Try to imagine their crestfallen surprise, surprise for all of us, when we pulled up at the main gate of the new camp and found a whole big bunch of women from Trieste just standing there, waving their handkerchiefs (Yoo-hoo!). Somehow, and easily enough, they had found out our Top Secret destination and, overcoming all obstacles and boundaries, beaten us there. I'm telling you there were some long faces and faint smiles in the trucks.

3.

Barring some major crime involving American GIs, and even in that case they will work mainly as liaison with and for the local Austrian police, the actual duties of these two soldiers are more in the line of courtesy patrol than anything else. They will patrol the town, check various well-known bars and public places, looking for GIs who are drunk or disorderly. Most of these, if any and if possible, they will not arrest but will simply carry back to the barracks. They will correct uniform violations. They may spot-check for ID cards, passes, and papers. Mostly they will be a visible and symbolic presence of the American intention to maintain some kind of good order. Mostly, except for the boredom, it is good, clean duty and not a bad way to pass the time.

Once in town they check in on the basic radio network, linking themselves, more or less and depending on the equipment, to the camp, to the local Austrian police, and to the other patrols. They stop briefly at the station of the local police. Who are friendly enough and who are not, at this time, holding any GI under arrest for anything. These would have to be taken back to the camp and the stockade there.

Now they can take a turn or two slowly driving up and

down some of the main streets, then they will go down to the bridge across the Danube and the checkpoint on our side. There are two conventional checkpoints, one on each side, American and Russian.

The 12th Field has drawn the duty, for this month, of manning the American checkpoint, so our pair on patrol stop by to say hello to some guys from the outfit. Theoretically there is, by treaty, free access for troops both ways. We can go across the Russian zone into the Four Power City of Vienna on the train, the Mozart Express, with American flags painted on the cars and with soldiers armed with grease guns guarding each car. And, with a proper pass, American soldiers can cross the bridge and pass through the Russian checkpoint and vice versa. Every day or so this right is tested. A vehicle of some kind will be sent across to the other side. After passing the checkpoint the vehicle, having scored its legal point, will turn around and come back. The two soldiers in the Jeep might be asked to do this by the lieutenant on duty. But they are not; a truck went over and back this morning. They are relieved. It can be a . . . touchy situation. The Russians are, to us, very strange sometimes. Once, not long ago, for whatever reason, they suddenly closed the checkpoint and barred an American military truck at gunpoint. Because the bridge is narrow the driver had to back his way to our side again. Our lieutenant called in, according to his strict instructions, to his commanding officer. And the news went all the way up the mysterious chain of command. After a while a Russian Jeep came roaring up to their checkpoint: driver, Russian officer, two enlisted men in the back. Out jumped the officer, who conferred briefly with the other Russian officer on duty there. They drew their pistols and shot the two soldiers who were guarding the checkpoint. At which point the two enlisted men jumped out of the Jeep, removed the weapons and equipment from the dead guards, and—one, two, three, heave-ho!—threw their bodies off the bridge and into the Danube. Whereupon the new guards took up positions at the barrier.

The funny part (can you believe there is a funny part?) is this. When the young and green American lieutenant saw what was happening he drew his pistol, shouted at his own men to follow him, and raced across the bridge to . . . to do what? He had just witnessed a crime, no question. But, pistol or no pistol, outrage or not, it was a double murder well outside his jurisdiction. The Russian officers were sympathetic to his feelings but nonetheless amused. In halting English they tried to explain that somebody had to be punished for the mistake of closing the checkpoint to our right of access. They pointed out that the two soldiers, whose bodies had long since vanished in the flow of the river, were only Mongols (as were the two new replacements) and wouldn't be missed by anyone. Anyway, there were millions more where they came from.

My own firsthand experience came from having to instruct my unit in the Russian use of land mines and booby traps. It was supposed to be an area of my expertise. I knew a little, mostly self-taught, but not much. But nothing had prepared me for the chaotic and totally irrational ways and means of the Russian army with land mines. Every other army in the world (for many good reasons) makes and uses mines for specific purposes. For example, an antitank mine won't go off when a man walks over one. Maybe they have changed now, and I hope so, but in those days a cat, probably a mouse, could set off any Russian land mine. That's kind of crazy. Then there is the matter of the big bang. Every other army in the world uses mines that contain enough explosives, and no more, to do the job they are intended for. The Russkies had mines that, stepped on by one man (or one mouse), would blow up a whole football field. To what purpose? Terror, I reckon. Except that a combat soldier with any experience at all is not going to be terrified by a bigger bang. It's the death he fears, not the noise of it. Another example. In every other army in the world only fairly high-ranking officers, usually of field grade, can authorize laying down a mine field. It must be mapped and is usually clearly marked. The danger of it to one's own troops outweighs any value of intense secrecy. In the Russian army, in those days at least, a squad leader, a corporal or a sergeant, could lay mines anywhere without telling anyone and without mapping or marking them. In combat they often had to leave them right where they were, unseen or unknown, when they advanced or fell back. This didn't slow up the Germans much, but nobody will venture a guess as to how many Russians were blown up in World War II by their own mines. Huge numbers. No matter. Plenty more where they came from.

Today experts sometimes wonder why the Russians have built missiles with huge, "dirty" warheads, many megatons beyond any remotely conceivable destructive value or purpose. Counterproductive in the sense that they will create enormous dangers for their own people in the fallout. It makes no sense, but it is the same philosophy they had with land mines and Mongols.

We shoot the breeze with the guys at the checkpoint for a few minutes. Then we head back into Linz.

"Hey, let's get something to eat," the corporal says.

"Suits me."

———

4.

Everywhere the 12th Field went we had our special hideouts. In Trieste we had a hole in the wall called the Poker Bar. Here we found and laid claim to the *Gasthaus* of the little farm village of Leonding, a few miles outside of Linz and close by the rifle range, an old one going back to the bright and colorful Austro-Hungarian Empire days. Which is how we found it in the first place, marching out there to fire qualification on our M-1s and carbines. A big, sprawling place (large for such a small village), quiet, dark, low-ceilinged, a kind of cave with a long wooden bar and with huge round waxed oak tables. Here we held our battery party a couple of weeks ago—plenty of booze, a show all the way from Germany with a stripper, a couple of female acrobats, a magician, and a trained-dog act.

Some of us did skits for the show, too. Mine was the only one that called for a costume. Just before we did our little skit, I was to slip back to the room the Germans were using as a dressing room and change into my homemade clown costume. When the moment for me to go and get ready arrived, I was more than slightly drunk and bitterly disappointed, too, that I was going to have to miss the striptease.

For a moment it seemed to me that I had been waiting patiently for that particular striptease for my whole life. You know how a drunk thinks. I had done my duty, but nonetheless I was going to have to miss the whole thing. Saddened to the marrow of my bones, profoundly pissed off, I went back and found the room where everybody (with no privacy at all) was busily dressing and undressing, putting on makeup, etc.

Somehow I let everyone there know how bitterly disap-

pointed I was to have to miss the stripteaser's performance. I
may even have told her, for she was just leaving the dressing
room when I came in—a tiny, dark-haired woman of inde-
terminate age (not young), layered in a gauzy, sequined black
costume.

Inside the dressing room we could hear the bump-and-
grind music playing, hear also the shouts and cheers of the
battery, while I put on my clown costume and makeup, then
sat, disconsolate, on a stool, refusing to be cheered up by the
young and amazingly attractive female acrobats. Who were
lively and sympathetic and who were also (though I wouldn't
even notice this at the time; only hours later, back at the
barracks, would it dawn on me) as sleekly naked as golden
apples on a bough. More so than the exotic dancer ever allowed herself to be. Nothing they said or did could cheer me
up much. Not even when they slipped on their bathrobes and
came out to watch my own amateur clown act. And then
applauded and were wonderfully supportive. Even helping
me out of my costume and makeup.

I remember this with mild embarrassment, but mostly for
what it tells me about male (my own) psychology. How much
of it, the dancing life of Eros, is in the head. How much even
memory can be fantasy.

Here, though, out of the brightness of the spring afternoon we stand at the bar eating Holstein *Schnitzel*s, the ones
with a couple of fried eggs on top, and drinking frosty steins
of beer. The *Schnitzel*s are fine here and so is the venison the
Austrians serve with a wine sauce. We are standing, trying to
preserve our khakis from wrinkles. There are a few old guys
playing cards at one table, nothing more going on.

We bullshit with the owner, who is really not much older
than we are, though he looks a generation older. He speaks

good English. He fought the Russians in the East and then was a prisoner in Siberia. We swap army stories. Our guys have mixed feelings about the Krauts, but everybody respects them as soldiers. He is telling us about how his father, who is still alive, and even some of these old card players still remember Hitler, who lived in Leonding as a child. Hitler's father was a customs officer who had owned a farm and lost it and moved into the village when Hitler was about six years old. The boy would come to the *Gasthaus* in the evening and get a bucket of draft for his father's supper. They can remember that. They remember, too, how he used to whistle, coming and going. He could whistle tunes very well, they say.

He would come into this same room and stand, right here in the same place where we are standing, waiting to get his bucket of beer. A funny feeling for us now.

We like this *Gasthaus* because they treat the guys from the 12th Field well here. Even our very few black soldiers in the only-newly integrated American army. Other places, especially in the city, are not so friendly to black soldiers. Once they go to a place it gets a name and none of the locals will go back there. And they shun the whores who go with black soldiers. We don't care one way or the other what the locals do. Except where it concerns our own outfit. There is no color line in the 12th Field.

While we stand there eating, stuffing our faces with good food, he tells us how (he believes) he survived in the labor camp in Siberia. By counting calories and judging and doling out energy. Most of the time they lived on soup. The whole trick was to try to gain energy from the soup, not to spend more getting it than a serving of soup contained. It was always a matter of energy, not hunger. People who didn't know any better ran and jostled and wrestled each other for extra helpings when there were any, using up far more energy in the process than they would ever gain. They filled their bellies and they died sooner than the rest.

We nod with straight-faced understanding as we wolf the veal and eggs and swallow the rich, sweet, delicious local beer.

It is not that we are utterly insensitive. But we are young and strong and (as yet) undefeated. We cannot seriously imagine surrendering to anybody.

5.

More than thirty years later the sergeant, now a professor pushing on toward retirement, will write a poem about that very afternoon in that *Gasthaus*. It will, inevitably, being a part of memory and recollection, be slightly different, at least in focus and emphasis, from what I have already been telling you. But, nevertheless, it is part of the picture. The *moving picture,* if memory is a kind of movie.

Here is the poem:

Some Enormous Surprises
Not many may now remember,
fewer and fewer remember,
most because they never knew
in the first place, being lucky
or too young, and others
because they are too few and too old
already, but anyway, I remember

the three reasons most often advanced
in those innocent days before the War
as strong and self-evident argument

that Adolf Hitler was crazy.
First, that he was a strict vegetarian.
Second, that he did not smoke or permit
any smoking around him, being convinced

that smoking cigarettes was somehow
linked to lung cancer.
Third, because he went around saying
that the Volkswagen, laughable beetle,
was a car of the future.
Maybe God, in all His power and majesty,
can still enjoy the irony of it.

Miles later, young man, old soldier, I
stand at the bar of a *Gasthaus*
in Leonding, country village near Linz,
lean against the dark, smooth, polished wood,
drinking and listening to very old men
remembering the days of the Austro-Hungarian Empire.
Happens that Hitler's father lived here then.

And they can remember him and his son, too,
who every evening came to this *Gasthaus*
for a bucket of beer for his father's supper.
Would stand there patiently waiting where
you are standing now, then, pail in hand,
set off under early stars along a lane
toward the lights of home, whistling in the dark.

Everyone who knew agrees that then and later
he was a wonderful whistler, worth listening to.
I lean back against the bar to picture
how he was then, lips puckered,
whistling tunes I do not know,

beer rich and foamy, sloshing in the pail,
smells of wood smoke, cooking meat, and cabbage.

And, invisible and implacable, always
the wide smile of God upon His creatures, one and all,
great and small, among them this little pale-faced boy,
for whom He has arranged some enormous surprises,
beyond any kind of imagining, even myself,
drunk in this place, years from home, imagining it.

6.

Now then, full of good food and beer and full of goodwill
toward humankind, one and all, our two soldiers have driven
into town, parked their Jeep in a reserved space, and are taking a stroll around the *Bahnhof.* They will check the papers
of a few GIs who are arriving and departing. They will cau-
tion a soldier or two to button up a shirt pocket or tighten
up a necktie. And they will watch the trains come and go.
The weather is really fine and dandy, couldn't be better. Nice
and warm and getting warmer with the afternoon. The air is
scented with springtime. Or is it the little bouquets of flowers
so many people seem to be carrying? The girls are in their
light dresses already. Splendid, if a little pale from winter.
Sap stirs in the limbs of the sergeant and the corporal.

Unusually crowded today. They are separated by the
crowds. No matter. They will meet up sooner or later on one
of the platforms or back at the Jeep.

Alone, I stroll, not strut, out of the great barn of a building (most GIs call it the Barnhof) into the sunlight on a platform. People, crowds of them, smiling and jabbering, waiting
for a train. Even if my German were good enough to

understand more than a few rudimentary phrases, I could not hear what they are saying. Somewhere nearby, though I can't yet see it, a brass band is playing cheerful oompah music. Deafening and delightful.

Must be a local holiday of some kind. Now I am closer to the band. I see the middle-aged musicians, their cheeks chipmunking as they play. I am standing close by the huge bass drum. Which keeps a steady rhythm.

This band is of an age that would allow them to have played all through the war. I wonder if they did that.

Now, even as I hear the shrill scream of the whistle, I see all the faces in the crowd turn toward the track where the train is coming slowly, with sighs of steam, easing into the station. To my amazement I see their faces, all of them, change entirely in a wink of time. A moment ago they were animated, smiling. Now each mask of flesh is anxious and searching. And, as if at an order, they all begin to cry. I have never been among a huge crowd of weeping people before. Sobs and tears all around me. Stunned and lost, I feel; out of empathy (and perhaps out of a military reflex), tears well up in my own eyes. I am one of them, I am one with them, though I do not know why.

Now many in the crowd are holding up enlarged photographs, placards with names printed large on them. Like some kind of grotesque parody of a political rally.

The doors open, and out of the train, helped by porters, many of them with crude canes and crutches, here come, one after another, a ragged company of dazed, shabby, skinny scarecrows. They are weeping also, some of them. Others study the crowd, searching with hard looks and dry eyes for familiar faces. The band is deafening. Next to me the bass drum pounds and pounds in tune and in time with my heart.

In time, very soon, in fact, I will learn that they are the latest contingent of Austrian veterans from the Eastern Front, returning home from Siberia. The Russians are moving slowly, in their own inexorable, patient, glacial fashion, toward a treaty here in Austria (as I will learn much later), if not a war first. Part of that movement is to let some of the scarecrows who have somehow managed to survive until now come home.

But here and now I know nothing of that and care less. I see a homecoming of the defeated and the wounded. Some greeted with great joy, with flowers and embracing. Some, as always, alone now even at home—though I see schoolchildren have been assigned the duty of making sure that everyone gets a greeting and some flowers.

I stand there knowing one thing for certain—that I am seeing our century, our time, close and truly. Here it is and, even among strangers, I am among them, sharing the moment of truth whether I want to or not.

An American sergeant stands in the swirling crowd with tears rolling down his cheeks. He will be gone from here soon, first miles, then years and years away. But he will not, because he cannot, forget this moment or himself in it, his share of this world's woe and joy, the lament and celebration of all living things.

Uncles
and Others

1.

A Confederate officer, himself as raggedy as a scarecrow, to-gether with a few of his men, most of them shoeless and all of them in tattered and torn and patched pieces of uniform, is on his hands and knees crawling down the long, straight rows of a cornfield. They all go very slowly, carefully, and as quietly as they can. Above all they do not want the farmer in the log cabin, perhaps a quarter of a mile away, to find them here. For what they intend to do, the farmer could have them hanged. It is a capital offense in this army, and the com-manding officer of these men would hang them one and all for the sake of a discipline that has not broken yet. But, you see, they are starving. Truly. Since yesterday or perhaps the day before they have had nothing to eat and drink but a handful of acorns and some muddy creek water. They have to risk hanging or die of starvation. Now, there are some skinny cows browsing a piece of pasture just beyond the edge of the cornfield. One, an old cow of not much use to anyone, is nearest the rows of corn. They plan to kill that cow. To cut it up and carry it off into the thick woods behind them, where, at a safe distance, they will build a little fire and cook the meat. Young as they are (and some of these are scarcely in their teens, and the officer, my great-grandfather, is not yet twenty-one), they are experienced and hardened veterans of the war. By now, fairly late in the war as it will prove to be, they do not pray or plan or hope anymore to live through to the end of it. That will happen or not happen. But, among many other ways and means, they would rather not have to die hungry.

You can understand that.

It seems to be all clear ahead. The old contented cow has moved even closer to the cornfield. There is not even a thin feather of white smoke coming from the cabin's chimney. No sounds. No dog around, thank God, to bark and bite. Farmer is somewhere else at work, in another direction. They are still crawling along down the corn rows when they hear something. Sound, unmistakable, of metal on metal. They hear that sound again, louder and somewhat closer. They freeze in place. Very slowly, even as a puff of light breeze teases the half-grown cornstalks, the officer turns his head to look in the direction the sounds came from. Light glints off something only a few rows away. It's a rifle barrel and another one. There are armed men, uniforms of dark blue, so close by he could pick up a clod of red clay earth and chunk it and hit them.

What next?

Holding his breath, he lowers his head and face to the earth. I lower mine, too, tasting, smelling the sweet odor of turned red clay in late springtime. I can hear the breeze rattling in the green cornstalks.

What next?

———

2.

The Elizabethans, my forebears, with whom I have visited for many years, had themselves a proverb for almost every situation and occasion. One that I have kept in mind, as if blazoned in neon, for *this* occasion is "There can be no play without a fool in it." Am I the fool of my own play? No good or happy answer to that question, but it led me toward a skinny and postmodern one of my own. Which might as well be "You can't write anything worth reading without an epigraph." And so here is my epigraph. It has at least the advantage of being economical, since it is in my own words. Of course I am fully aware of the dangers, even in autobiography, of depending on your own words. Wasn't it Raymond Chandler who said something undeniably wise like "When you use your own stuff for inspiration, you are already dead"? Something like that. Anyway, dead or alive, coming ready or not, here is my text in brief and in part, a short poem called "Main Currents of American Political Thought."

Main Currents of American Political Thought
Gone then the chipped demitasse cups
at dawn, rich with fresh cream and coffee,
a fire on the hearth, winter and summer,
a silk dandy's bathrobe, black Havana cigar.

Gone the pet turkey gobbler, dogs, and geese,
a yard full of chickens fleeing the shadow of a hawk,
a tall barn with cows and a plow horse, with corn,
with hay spilling out of the loft, festooning the dead
    Pierce Arrow.

Gone the chipped oak sideboards and table
heavy with plenty of dented, dusty silverware.

Gone the service pistol and the elephant rifle
and the great bland moose head on the wall.

"Two things," you told me once, "will keep
the democratic spirit of this country alive—
the free public schools and the petit jury."
Both of these things are going, too, now, Grandfather.

You had five sons and three daughters,
and they are all dead or dying slow and sure.
Even the grandchildren are riddled with casualties.
You would not believe these bitter, shiny times.

What became of all that energy and swagger
At ninety you went out and campaigned for Adlai
     Stevenson
in South Carolina. Half that age and I have to force
myself to vote, choosing among scoundrels.

3.

Autobiography, like any other form of confession, is finally,
if not first and foremost, a self-serving act. And what else
could it be? At its most sane and rational (that is, rarely enough)
the autobiographical impulse is most often a cry for mercy
concealed as a nonnegotiable demand for justice. What it
amounts to, then, is copping a plea. And even on its other,
darker side, for the sake of whatever kinds of dark hungers
and satisfactions, autobiography remains much closer to the
rhetoric of fiction than to any objective arrangement of hard
facts. It is a matter of aesthetics most of all. And in any case
there are some strict limits to our contemporary shapes and
forms of pleading. When *The Book of Common Prayer*'s latest
version of the old "General Confession" dropped the image

of erring and straying lost sheep, presumably for the sake of a more sophisticated urbanity, and cut as well (among other things) the acknowledgment of ourselves as being "miserable offenders" and the outright admission that "there is no health in us," all this added up to something more than the simple and direct expression of the widespread contemporary desire to deal with God on some basis of equality. It also represented a shift in the point of view of the praying narrator. And so I ask you. When even our prayers partake of the art and craft of fiction, why should autobiography be subjected to vulgar claims of credibility?

And Southern autobiography has some other, special problems. It is at least perceived by others as consisting of more things to confess and to conceal. And even disallowing that notion—as I do, now and forever, though I recognize that it is widely held by many, at least some of whom do themselves small honor and less justice by that kind of reflexive self-indulgence—even ignoring that problem, there is still the matter of manners. It is generally thought, among my Tribe, to be an infraction, a taboo, an exhibition of bad manners to present oneself in any form that is radically different from the expectations of others. Because this is so, who knows, ever, how much of what passes for Southern autobiography and humble confession is not, instead, purely and simply the exercise of social charm?

I, myself, am the books I have written, the works, large or small, into which I have poured my life, my self, as carefully and awkwardly as pouring from one bottle into another. In that sense I am to be found, the life of me, in my work. But this is no kind of news. It is true of every writer, living or dead, whom I admire and respect and envy. The best of them held back very little. The best of all held back nothing at all and, in the end, were merely and enviably dry husks in the wind.

My autobiography is in my words and fables, though I must admit it has taken me most of a lifetime to recognize the simple truth of that and I must also admit that much that is clear enough to me now will always be inaccessible to others. Which means, I reckon, that my life is written and printed in an unknown tongue. I seriously doubt that anyone, besides myself, could get to the bottom of it.

And I do believe I am something more than the facts and events of my days. I do not mean to belittle the things that have happened to me or to make light of the things I have done that I ought not to have done and the things I have left undone that I ought to have done. But I do think that these things cannot mean very much to others. Probably should not mean much to others. Unless I were laying claim—which I am not—to a public life of great actions and events or even a closeness to such things.

I propose something else. The ancient and honorable image of the pebble in water that instantly vanishes but proves its existence by the slow spreading of concentric circles around an empty center. In addition to our works—which are there to be judged (or ignored) now or later—and in addition to the thin staining coat of facts and dates that is our reduced being, we are also all of those around us, our friends and enemies, those whom we love and hate. And we are also those we were given at birth, those we were given to, like it or not. We are our family, our Tribe. And that is what I am thinking of here and now. Autobiography not precisely as a matter of inheritance, nor as a ritual matter of tribal totem and taboo, but, anyway, as a matter of the self defined by blood, by kinship, by others who are not chosen, like friends or enemies, but *given* all at once, like it or not, like the mysterious gifts of some fairy godmother, benign or malevolent, at a christening or wedding.

When I talk of the uncles and others around me, mostly ghosts already, I am also speaking of myself. From what they were I begin to learn who I am, where I have been, and even, sometimes, why all these things are so.

The same is, of course, true of you and you, all of you, all of us. The lives of our blood kin are fables we are entitled to enter and inhabit.

4.

Who are the uncles? Let us settle that right now. On my mother's side of the family there are her five brothers, from the eldest, Bill, named for his father, and including, in order, Courtney, Fred, Jack, and Chester. Bill was old enough to have been in the cavalry before the First World War. Chester is young enough to have served in the Tank Destroyers in World War II.

My father had two younger brothers, Oliver and Legh. I never knew Legh at all except in photographs. Because he died before I was born. He was a mountain climber and a professional guide who disappeared forever (on Mount Washington? Mount Rainier? I cannot remember and nobody is handy here and now to ask) in a sudden and unseasonal snowstorm. There was more of that once upon a time in America. People just vanished. Oliver came home, highly decorated, from the First World War to become first a newspaperman in New York, and an outstanding one; then, when silent pictures gave way to talkies, a Hollywood screenwriter. Very well—mountain climber and screenwriter on one side.

On the other, Fred was a musician, Courtney was (among other things) a minor-league baseball player, Jack was an outstanding PGA golfer, and Chester was a dancer, in Broadway musicals, in nightclubs around the world, and on the great ocean liners.

Whatever else, you can see that, by the time I and others of the next generation came along, there was no special notice, neither blame nor shame, in the modest ambition to be a writer. There were writers already on the Garrett side, my Aunt Helen, who wrote wonderful children's books, and my Uncle Oliver. A great-uncle, Harry Stillwell Edwards, of Macon, Georgia, on the other side, a writer who won some prizes in the late nineteenth century, earned some money, and whose late short novel of Reconstruction, *Aneas Africanus,* sold a couple of million copies and remains quietly in print to this day.

Nobody would even notice another writer.

In fact, if you think about it seriously (which none of us, in fact, did), being a writer was slightly more conventional and respectable, if a lot less rewarding, than what the majority of the uncles were up to. Certainly less adventurous. True, my mother's father and my own were lawyers, and very good ones, but, each in his own way, flamboyant performers in life and profession, trial lawyers when the give-and-take of the Southern courtroom, equally urgent and dramatic in large matters and the smallest of things, was still one of the chief forms of entertainment and principal sources of public language in the South. My father had intended to have another kind of life. Went to MIT to be a mining engineer, ran out of money, and became instead a miner himself in the far West, becoming finally a charter member of the United Mine Workers. Then, partly crippled by accidents and by disease, made his way back home to Florida to some cousins there, aiming to go to South America. Became a lawyer in Florida instead.

His father-in-law, my grandfather, originally from Charleston and McClellanville, South Carolina, was a licensed nautical pilot before he became a lawyer, drove his own trotters and pacers in high-stakes horse races. Served for a time as solicitor general of Georgia and ran, unsuccessfully, for governor of Florida. I did not see him at his richest and most extravagant—the days when, for example, he had a ninety-foot steam yacht, the *Cosette,* as fast and nimble as anything in the Atlantic Ocean, which with a minimal professional crew and his five sons he handled himself. But I did see him in a couple of fine old houses that he managed from the front porch with a nineteenth-century military megaphone. And later, too, when all his space was a rented room in the back of the post office of Naples, North Carolina, and later still in a plain and simple cottage next to the Inland Waterway in McClellanville, where he died.

I remember his sister, Aunt Mamie, who had once enjoyed the society of Charleston, living, at her end, with a tall and solemn mountain man, Uncle Tom, who always wore bib overalls, in a dirt-floor log cabin, far gone in the North Carolina mountains. A well for water and an outdoor privy, and candles and kerosene for light. Spare and sparse and wonderfully neat and clean. Old family silver gleamed on the crude and sturdy table where we ate (in summertime) cornbread and fresh vegetables and wild roots and berries, and mysterious and gamey stews; for Uncle Tom was a constant, seasonless hunter in the woods. It was, to me, an altogether happy place. Uncle Tom taught me to shoot and to fish the mountain streams and where to find the best blackberries and how to kill and clean and pluck a chicken. He also taught me how to milk and to plow, too, with one mule or two horses. Aunt Mamie seemed altogether happy, too. Couldn't have been more so when she had lived with her first, handsome husband in a house on the Battery in Charleston.

All of them on both sides were what we would call high rollers, seriously and sincerely wild spenders, never taking money or the getting of it very seriously, often coming into money somehow, yet never seeking it for its own sake, never doing things (or selling anything except themselves) at the expense of others to get it. They all had honor as an ideal, and acted honorably. And they gave away, in common Christian charity, as much as they spent, for service to others and to the community, the larger Tribe, was an unquestionable duty. They were often called generous by others, when they had the means to give, and gave freely to the less fortunate and the disabled and disadvantaged, but they did not think of themselves as doing anything more (or less) than their bounden duty. The American Dream (not an expression I ever heard from them or anyone else except politicians) had nothing to do with upward or downward mobility. It had to do with honor and liberty and fairness (equity). When they were well-to-do they lived well. When they were poor they worked hard at hard and menial jobs. They worked with hard hands and without shame. They could, therefore, afford to be poor and proud. Which is just as well, because that is how most of them ended up, dirt-poor in some cases, not in self-pity or spoken regret, but rich in memories, anyway, and the laughter of recapitulation, stories of fat times still preserved and repeated in the lean and plain, and, at the end, in what we would choose to call abject poverty. Fred, for instance, who as a pianist had sometimes accompanied well-known singers and solo artists, was a hermit and literally a beachcomber when he died. When asked what he wanted, all he asked for was a set of teeth. Which he was given. Chester, who had made thousands of dollars a week as a dancer, deep in the heart of the depression, came home from World War II to find himself too old and battered and his way of dancing out of fashion. Went through some bad times in New York before he got a job teaching at the newly founded Arthur Murray's. Where (his luck was always pretty good) he sold two lifetime courses to a very rich, good-looking and recently divorced heiress, then married her, and they have lived happily ever after since. On the other side, Oliver, in spite of several glamorous and very expensive wives, was about as rich as a Hollywood screenwriter can be. But when he died of a heart attack in a laundry across the street from his hotel, he was listed by the New York City Police, who took him to the morgue, as "Unidentified Laborer."

Pride and honor mattered, but mainly as a matter of style, which in turn says that what is outward and visible, be it ever so bright and beautiful, be it ever so delightful, rich, or strange, is only costuming and camouflage. What is inward and spiritual is what truly and deeply matters. And it has nothing to do, really, with success or failure, good luck or bad.

I suppose this Tribal code was good training for a writer, an American writer in our century.

It was good training for them, too. Because some of them were wonderful, truly wonderful, at what they did. Chester was a superb dancer who for a time had other dancers, including even the great Fred Astaire, billed under him. You have never heard of him, that's for sure. Or of my Uncle Jack either, though he won many a golf tournament, early and very late in his life, and a couple of times was a single stroke,

one putt, away from the absolute top. Other professionals remember him, the old-timers. "Jack was the greatest golfer I
ever saw," they usually tell me. But in an instant they are
laughing and telling stories of bets he made and won or lost,
all the tricks and jokes he pulled.

And only a true cinema buff, an antiquarian, would know
about Oliver H. P. Garrett, though he wrote well over one
hundred feature films, founded and was first president of the
Screenwriters Guild, and wrote (and is now, at last, finally
credited with it) the final shooting script of *Gone with the
Wind.*

There were virtues among the Tribe also—good manners, bestowed equally to all, regardless of station or status.
How could we do otherwise? That bum or bag lady could
just as well be one of us. There was an easy generosity. They
withheld nothing from each other or, indeed, from anybody
else who was not an overt enemy. Anyone who was an enemy, however, found them implacable, ruthless, passionately
violent, and finally, in victory, magnanimous. Some of the
Tribe, early and late, came to violent ends.

You could not, ever, even consider the notion of betrayal,
of betraying any one of our own or any word or promise we
had made.

Who taught us these things? you will justly ask. Who
were the keepers of Tribal history, the custodians of the Tribal
lore, the Tribal virtues?

The women, of course. The aunts. They kept and tended
the flames. And they made things easy for the uncles. Who
would not easily have dared to act any differently than they
did.

Nor do I.

What are our vices? There is a pleasant laziness that often

eases into a well-developed habit of procrastination. We tend to embrace the rigors of self-discipline (upon which our powers and virtues much depend) by fits and starts. And by the same token we have a tendency to become addicted to all kinds of bad habits. There were and are too many drunks in the Tribe. Some are truly, greatly gifted, but they often take their gifts lightly and for granted, as if anything more than lighthearted acceptance would be corrupting. More seriously, although they are tolerant, even egalitarian, in their attitudes toward others, they can be very hard on their own. Within the Tribe the casualty rate—dead, wounded, and crazy—is high. And although they are at once generous and compassionate, they are also damnably proud (if pushed to be so) and dangerously violent if challenged. Once challenged and fully engaged, they have been known to bear grudges over amazing distances of time and space, carefully cupped like water in their hands.

On the one hand this is a source of shame and guilt, because they are Christians and uneasy in their hatred. But, at one and the same time, in the secular world we all have to live and die in, it means they can still be outraged by injustice or atrocity (at a time when, if you think about it, so few of us still are . . . at least for long). It renders our Tribe more or less unfit for modern corporate life and the contemporary wisdom that anything under the sun is, finally, negotiable. Difficult for them, the uncles and others; but for a writer, to be given a constant duplicity like that as a birthright is a great gift, even the continued inner conflict of it. Never quite to belong, outside the Tribe, may not be comfortable, but it is helpful to the craft of fiction and especially so in a time of ethical clichés and stereotypes like our own.

Is there—has there been any magic among us? Not much,

I reckon. Some ghosts in the times gone by when ghosts walked about more freely. An aunt who could tell fortunes, by one means and another, with either amazing accuracy or amazing luck, as the case may be. Dreams and visions. In my childhood, no death or disaster in the family ever took our women by surprise. They felt it just before it was known.

The aunts on both sides who were blood kin were formidable women, strong-willed, greatly gifted, sometimes difficult, if lighthearted. Some of the aunts by marriage were colorful enough. There was a German dancer who was one of Billy Rose's Long-Stemmed Roses and later with the circus. There was a Hungarian movie actress and even one wife, an aunt I never met, from Bali. The sisters, it seems, never seriously begrudged their brothers' marital adventures.

Adventure was what it was all about. Uncle Bill could tell a tale or two about flying in the Great War, but he always said (and I believe) that nothing in the world could ever equal the pure excitement of leading a troop of cavalry flat out in a full-gallop charge. Bugles, the sudden thunder of hooves directly behind you, and the open space before you as, saber drawn and pointed, you rode your mount to its limit of speed and endurance and rode yourself to the limits of your courage.

Sometimes the source of writing (for myself at least) is uneasiness, the conflict of opposing, often contradictory powers. You can see that belonging to our Tribe has often been an uneasy role. Especially when I was young and more painfully aware that there were many other tribes and people who thought and acted very differently than our own. At times it could be a burden, a sorrow even. It is another sort of tribal habit—from another tribe, the tribe of scribblers—in modern times to make more art from our wounds than from our blessings. I am as guilty of this as anyone. My family, my

Tribe, has appeared most directly in my poetry and short
stories. I have not been fair or even accurate except in the
summoning up of my own feelings. Which—true to my
Tribe—I try to do without flinching.

Here is a poem that is precisely about all that:

Child Among Ancestors
Dimensionless, they've left behind
buttons, daguerreotypes, a rusty sword
for a small boy to fondle, and the tales
he hears without believing a word

about the escapades of the tall people.
The tight-lipped men with their beards
and their unsmiling women share the glint
of unreality. The facts he's heard,

how this one, tamer of horses, fell
in a flourish of flags and groping dust,
and one met a dragon on the road,
and another, victim of his lust,

changed into a pig with a ring tail,
fail to convince or bear the burden of
flesh and his struggle for identity.
What he has never seen he cannot love,

though dutifully he listens.
Dismissed, he takes the sword and goes
campaigning in garden and arbor,
and in the hen yard mighty blows

glisten in a tumult of feathers.
The hens cackle like grown-ups at tea

as he scatters them to the four winds.
The rooster, ruffled, settles in a tree

and crows an ancient reprimand.
Let them stand up to me, the boy
thinks. Let them be tall and terrible
and nothing less than kings. His joy

is all my sadness at the window
where I watch, wishing I could warn.
What can be said of the dead? They rise
to make you curse the day that you were born.

5.

One way and another, poorly or sometimes very well, we
were, one and all, for as far back as I can learn, engaged in
what were (at least then) known as manly things—hunting
and fishing; horses and boats; physical sports, which if not
always "contact" sports were always anyway the most risky
and dangerous we could practice. Gambling, with money and
things, of course, but also with hide and hair and heart, was
good. To win was pleasure, to be sure, but losing was seldom
a serious pain (good gamblers shrug it off and bet again as
soon as they can). And losing was never a shame unless you
had played things safely, withheld, been miserly with energy,
been stingy with the exposure of self. Victory was, could be
sweet enough, but not as a gloating triumph when it was
earned over the full and honorable expense and effort of the
defeated, of a beaten equal. In our Tribe we would no more
have danced in the brief, bright end zone of joy of victory
over a worthy enemy than we would have danced or pissed
on the grave of a friend.

What you can see is that, whatever else, we were well prepared for war. Which is just as well, because we fought in all the wars, from even before this was a nation until here and now. Not often as professional soldiers and sailors (of whom there were always a few among us, whose vocation was somehow as vaguely contemptible as it seemed unnecessary), but nevertheless as soldiers and sailors in our country's wars—and thus in every generation from the beginning.

There are some things—simply left over, never preserved—from the old days. A rusty Civil War sword, a toasting fork presented by General Washington to an officer who served him for a time. Various and sundry kinds of brass buttons and insignia. From later, from our own century, crossed rifles of the infantry, crossed sabers of the cavalry, crossed cannons of the field artillery, my Uncle Bill's wings as a flyer in the First World War. And more than these things, there have been voices, people to listen to, from my great-grandfather from Appalachicola, Florida, who fought out the long brutal years in the West, on down through the youngest cousins who fought and were wounded in Vietnam. We have all served our time. From them all came the gift of their stories, alike only in that they were always the kinds of stories told by combat veterans. Which is to say, seldom if ever directly concerned with any kind of combat, or even suffering, but instead the exemplary anecdote, sometimes funny and almost always ironic. And usually paradoxical. Which is to say, even the most innocent and inexperienced of us, thanks to Tribal history, arrived wherever we were sent, that is wherever we had to go, almost without expectations or illusions. Which, in turn, means that we were usually spared the common experience of disillusionment. Our concentration was not upon a Cause or Causes or any other abstractions, which we

deemed (long before we read any novels about any of it) ir-
relevant, having seen and known that the fighting qualities of
soldiers, admirable or pathetic, have nothing at all to do with
the justice or injustice of the Causes they are thought to represent. I should mention the paradox that in civil life we are
often (as the first poem tried to say) passionate about political
affairs, if never quite able to hew to any particular party line,
and even though we do not, finally, believe that politics proves
or settles anything under the sun. That is, we are free to care
because it does not matter.

6.

Ideally, there ought to be illustrations in this book. In place
of those let imagination and memory join together to create
a slide show (or a sideshow) of illustrations.

Let us begin with portraits. I am thinking of those Brady
portraits, his and his contemporaries'. Thinking of those hard,
odd, genuinely eccentric and entirely individual faces, faces
that we would call wild, if not savage and barbarous, if we
did not already know many of the names that go with the
faces and the deeds that go with the names. It may well be—
it is at least a serious and debatable question—that American
society was somewhat more homogeneous then. But judging
by its recorded faces, we can easily surmise that, set against
our own, the general gene pool then allowed for much more
facial diversity and variety than the melting pot does now.
Something has happened to the American face, and in a very
short time. Is there a single Federal judge, coast to coast, who
has a face as expressive and even symbolic as that of the late
Judge Learned Hand?

Picture the famous profile of Major General William T.

Sherman, the one with his collar buttoned and all the brass buttons on his dark uniform shining; close-cropped hair; dark, full, thick beard; nose as sharp as an ax blade; one visible bright eye fixed in a thousand-yard stare; completely unsmiling. Summon up Grant and Lee, Jefferson Davis and Abraham Lincoln.

I know of only two contemporary faces to match any of the Civil War portraits—Shelby Foote's and Alexander Solzhenitsyn's: the latter having risen from the dead, one miracle from among uncounted and mostly unmourned millions, the former as the man who has lived longer and more closely with our Civil War ancestors than anyone else. Foote knows what they were looking for and looking at and what they saw.

Somehow the standard-issue American face has changed over from its apparent material of cut stone, poured bronze, or whittled hardwood into something else, something much like molded plastic or (on a bad day) Silly Putty. And smiling. Almost always smiling.

Solzhenitsyn noticed it right away and mentioned it, earning some boos in response, during his Harvard commencement address of 1978: "But the fight for our planet, physical and spiritual, a fight of cosmic proportions, is not a vague matter of the future; it has already started. The forces of Evil have begun their offensive—you can feel their pressure—and yet your screens and publications are full of prescribed smiles and raised glasses. What is the joy about?" Which observation appropriately reminds us of a greater and deeper change, the change of what is *behind* the faces of then and now, as much as we can perceive and translate the things those faces seem to be saying to us. Of course, we always assume that what we read in a face is what was intended, that faces are saying no more and no less than they want to. We tend to praise and blame them for these very things. Knowing full well that it is an enormous untruth, an outrageous assumption. Knowing that no one alive, except perhaps a consummate professional actor, fully knows or is responsible for the expression of his face. And it is worth keeping in mind that the art of the actor is a mimetic derivation from the probably uncontrolled and irresponsible expression of authentic emotions by real people. But we judge anyway, being a litigious and pharisaical generation of self-appointed judges. Judging ourselves gently enough, if not with very much mercy or charity. And judging these others, the dead, with an Old Testament rigor.

We do seem to feel compelled to judge our personal past, just as we do severely judge America's past and the South's, especially when family is involved and extends over several generations. Generations that openly embraced very different values from our own. Generations we regularly acknowledge as having been, in many things, ignorant, insensitive, and wrongheaded. We judge and condemn them, or we apologize for them and hope to establish that we have improved and are better than they were, the scales fallen away from our eyes at last. This is such a common stance that I can't think of an autobiographical piece in recent years that does not (somehow) assume it.

Or we try to escape the problem by depicting our ancestors as innocent and lovable comedians.

I am not going to apologize for any of the values my family and ancestors may or may not have held. I am not going to apologize—or make light of—the things they did that they ought not to have done and the things they left undone that they ought to have done. If I were being facetious, I would argue that the contemporary celebration of cultural relativism ought to be extended at least far enough so as to include the dead. One of the characteristics of our secular society is the assumption that the living have not only the right but the duty to exhume and even desecrate the dead. Saint Augustine was not strictly talking theology when he asserted his belief that the dead are beyond our capacity to wound or bless, to praise or blame. And that—best news of all—there is not and never has been any evidence that the dead *care* one way or the other what we may think of them. Their attention seems to be focused elsewhere.

Well, in any case, we shall all be able to test the validity of his observations sooner or later, soon enough, won't we?

Recently in the *New York Times Book Review* the point was made that Jefferson Davis never apologized for the Civil War, as, evidently, he should have. How do you suppose he would have framed his apology?

My family fought on both sides in that war, and I knew some of those veterans in the flesh, by touch and by voice. As far as I know none of them apologized for it either.

And I am afraid I lack the necessary self-esteem to apologize on their behalf.

Hand in glove with the contemporary rush to judgment is the high-fever, hallucinatory joy of historical and personal guilt, self-righteousness turned inside out to display a wonderfully shrugging, worldlier-than-thou attitude that is sometimes confused by ignorant or innocent others as a posture of care, concern, compassion. I, too, must bear my burden of contemporary guilt like a student's obligatory backpack. But I flatly refuse to add to it one ounce, one feather's weight, of *historical* guilt for anything. I am not guilty of or for the actions of anyone but myself. Much that is autobiographical purports to be confession. I have yet to read any modern confession, in prose or in poetry, that is not so buttressed with mitigation and extenuation as to seem, finally, to ask more for reward than punishment, that is not more a plea for love and understanding than a hope for judgment and forgiveness.

Still and all, dead and living faces do speak to us. Sometimes, as in the familiar Tudor court portraits by Holbein, the Elizabethan miniatures by Hilliard, they are, to our eyes, so masklike and enigmatic as to speak only of mysteries in an unknown tongue. Sometimes, as in those Brady photographs, they do communicate some things clearly enough, some things in common. As different as they are from each other, those faces reveal an assumption that life is tragic and that pain, outward and inward, is accurately believed to be a constant companion. They reveal the wish to be seen and known as courageous, strong enough to endure much, brave enough to seek to bear the best and worst without any wincing.

Above all they do not wish to be taken as silly, foolish, laughable, or even as mainly clever. Wisdom and not shrewdness is their professed ideal. They do not plead for the love of perfect strangers. Look at the portraits of Henry James. Or even those of Walt Whitman, that great poet (and often profoundly silly man), who was surely wild for the love and admiration of strangers. See how easily he fell into the proper pose of his period. Consider that not one poet alive can even manage to make those expressions, not on a bet.

Something happened to our faces as we moved into this century. You can see it, conservatively enough, in the official faces of our presidents. Wilson, Harding, Coolidge even, though they already wore our own physiognomy, kept at the expression of hard seriousness they inherited from their fathers. Hoover began to soften into inexplicable cheerfulness. And then, finally, after Harry Truman, all of them, one and all, convey the foolish idea of wanting to be loved. Even Lyndon Johnson, who might have managed some nineteenth-century expressions if he had only known how. Next to our late-twentieth-century presidents, on the strength of faces alone, Rutherford B. Hayes, the nineteenth, and Benjamin Harrison, the twenty-third, for example, look like giants of the earth.

What is the message of the new face, the latest version? Think of our best and brightest poets and novelists. Then go well beyond the fragile arts and enter the worlds of the likes of Trump and Boesky, Iacocca and Icahn. It's all the same. Here are faces at once sly and shrewd (nobody would accuse them of expressing any wisdom except, perhaps, what used to be called worldly wisdom), ruthless and yet somehow sensitively vulnerable. Pitiless yet somehow self-pitying. There is an assertive weakness glossing over a dedicated and self-centered cruelty. They seem to beg for love and forgiveness even as they threaten to break your bones in two. And empty your pockets at the same time.

Contemporary man looks to be, by his own design and admission, a curious hybrid composed of almost equal parts of Woody Allen and General Manuel Antonio Noriega.

The faces of our public women are much harder for me to read. I remain as uncertain as Dr. Sigmund Freud, not only about what they want but also about what they really want us to think about them.

7.

My generation, call them the cousins, are widely scattered geographically. As well as in the South, we are now in Seattle and Santa Monica, Maine and Pennsylvania, New York City and New Hampshire. We are no longer likely to gather in full strength and number, even for weddings and funerals. This generation, however, remains Tribal. I am typical in the sense that I married into a family and tribe more or less like my own. Smaller and, in a sense, more distinguished. One that includes people like George Washington's Indian agent, Jasper Parrish, as well as (possibly) a famous Mohawk chief. Includes a prominent member of the Constitutional Convention—Nathaniel Gorham—and, even further back, the ship's carpenter on the *Mayflower*. Half of this family is Southern, too, coming out of Alabama. And it is a tribe with very similar values to our own, though more dignified, more calmly serious.

Much was probably wrong with old America and the early American colonists, and eager historians are busy telling us as much about their sins and follies as they can find out or imagine. But somehow, and simply, without special pride but without shame either, the old Americans created the place and above all the climate of social hope and political liberty that have attracted so many others from all over the face of the earth. This was their intention. This was their triumph. It cannot be revised away by anyone except a liar.

8.

We left my great-grandfather in a cornfield in Alabama or Georgia (most likely, in context, in Tennessee), having discovered that there were other armed men in those rows besides his own. Men in the blue uniforms of the enemy they had killed and who had tried to kill him and the others. What did he do? Well, from somewhere he produced a white handkerchief and, holding it, crawled among the Yankee soldiers until he met, face-to-face, his counterpart, a young

Yankee officer crawling toward him on his hands and knees. Face to face like bookends, they held a whispered negotiation. This was, as he was, beyond grudges. Both groups had the same aim and idea—that old cow browsing nearby. Both had the same essential fear—hanging for the crime if the farmer caught them at the business of killing and butchering his cow. The two young veteran officers were good soldiers and reasonable men. They made an arrangement to work together and to divide the meat half and half. And that they did, spending what was left of that day doing it. So that all the men of both groups were, for once, well fed, full, and satisfied, and lived to fight each other to the death on other days.

And he lived to hold me in his hands and on his lap and tell me that story.

And here and now I pass it along to you (like any other storyteller), claiming that I was there, even as I am here, and that at the center of the story there is something that speaks to you and me in the unknown tongue that we both can understand.

My Two
One-Eyed Coaches

Truth is, I have been writing all my life, at least for as long as I can remember, anyway, and well before I even knew how to write letters (or spell words) on a page. In our family we were all encouraged—encouraged? *we had to,* but, in fairness, it never occurred to any of us to want not to—to make up stories and poems and plays. And it became a fine and dandy way to spend an evening, in those lean and often happy depression years, unless there happened to be something good enough to cause us to give up our own devices and gather close around the tall Philco in the corner, in chairs and sitting on the floor, to look at its elegant cathedral shape and to study the mysterious lights glinting from deep within its secret places as we listened eagerly and attentively to the miracles of human voices and of sounds and music arriving in Orlando, Florida, out of thin, if usually hot and humid, air. Otherwise we very often wrote verses and stories and little plays, and then we presented them to each other before bedtime.

They derived, appropriately, from every kind of source—from events in our lives, from dreams and daydreams, from other stories, these latter sometimes from books or from each other's evening stories or, a bit later, from the Rialto Theater downtown, which cost a nickel for any child under twelve. And the same for some lucky children who were over twelve but didn't look it. Or were brazen enough to lie and get away with it. Or who were willing to scrunch down and try to look and act little.

Here's a coach for you, though not exactly one of the two I want to tell you about. If, at age twelve, you lost the right to go to the movies for a nickel—and we did, because my father was so absolute in integrity that he would not allow any of *us,* no matter what the rest of the world might be up to, to lie or cheat about anything large or small—you gained something else. You could then be a Boy Scout. Which I was. And, as a Boy Scout, one of the many things you could do was put on your uniform and go to Tinker Field and serve as an usher for the Rollins College football games. Which I did. In those days Rollins had a fine football team, too good for their league, really, and a wonderful football coach. Whose name has been lost to me forever by the years and wear and tear since then. Never mind. Nameless or not, he lives in my memory. After we had seated everyone, we could take a good seat (there were always plenty left) and watch the game ourselves. For free. I used to sit close behind the Rollins bench so I could see the players up close. And the thing that surprised me most then, and still astonishes me now, maybe more so since I have logged a lot of hours on benches both as a player and a coach, the astonishing thing was how quiet and calm and orderly the Rollins bench was. Nobody ever seemed to get upset or even very excited. The coach, in a coat and tie as I choose to remember him, sat quietly, like a disinterested spectator. Never raised his voice. Sometimes he would gesture, and a player would come over and kneel or hunker down in front of him. They would talk very quietly. Deadpan. You couldn't tell whether it was a situation of praise or blame.

I decided I wanted to be a coach like that and I wrote the man a letter, asking him please to tell me all about the profession of being a football coach. Back came a long and friendly and leisurely letter, treating my request seriously. A generous and warm letter. I have carried it with me for most of the rest of my life. It sits in the upper right-hand drawer of the desk in my boat house in York Harbor, Maine, even now. I wish it were here in Charlottesville so I could quote it to you.

I wish I could remember his name here and now. He was the last football coach Rollins College ever had, for they dropped football after World War II. His name has gone into my private dark with so many others, from schools and teams, from the army and graduate school and, yes, teaching. Even coaching. I can't for the life of me summon up the name of the head coach of football at Wesleyan University for whom I worked as an assistant line coach in the 1957 season. I can see his face clearly enough and remember him pacing up and down the sidelines, an older man, looking wise with experience and more intent than worried. Truth is, he was worried. Plenty. Sometimes in his pacing he would pause in front of me and ask in an urgent whisper: "What are they *doing* out there, Garrett? *What are they up to?*" It was a while before I allowed myself to realize that, late in his career, he had lost his learned sense of the order and coherence of the game. That it had, for him, returned to its original chaos and confusion. He knew the score but didn't have a clue what was happening or why. I now understand the feelings perfectly. I also understand the need to be a little furtive about sharing them.

Anyway, at twelve, briefly, I wanted to grow up and be a coach. And thanks to the coach at Rollins College I had at least some idea of what was involved. Of course, he had ruined me for one aspect of Real Life. After that I assumed that when you wrote somebody a letter, they answered. But when I was trying to learn to play the clarinet, I wrote Benny Goodman and he never answered. Neither did Joe Louis when I wrote him.

We will get back to coaches. But first I have to explain why it never occurred to me to need anyone else, outside of lifelong friends and my kinfolk, to encourage me toward reading and writing. I didn't look for what wasn't there. And soon enough the coaches—and not only my special and favorite and influential ones, but *all* of them, including a fair share of tyrants and incompetents—would make it brutally clear that no half-decent human being possessing a pair of functioning testicles would ever be caught, dead or alive, complaining about unpleasant, painful, and inevitably unfortunate things. I guess I owe them one and all, from the Delaney Street Grammar School kickball instructors to the coaching staff of Princeton University in the days of Charley Caldwell, the well-executed shrug of affected toughness I can offer, the run-it-out, get-up-and-shake-it-off-and-get-your-dead-ass-moving, the no-pain-no-gain philosophy that, I have to admit, didn't help me a whole lot on the playing fields to improve the level of my performance. But which, let me tell you, has enabled me to keep on trying to solve a lot of difficult problems.

What I was trying to say is that I came to reading and writing more or less naturally. As, for example, you might come to swimming early and easily. Which, matter of fact, I did, learning to swim at about the same time I learned to walk. And here's the irony of memory for you. I can very well remember the name of the man (he was the swimming coach at Rollins College) who took me as a toddler and threw me off the end of a dock into a deep lake where I had the existential choice of sinking or swimming. And chose to swim, thank you. His name was, I swear, Fleetwood Peoples. Could I forget a name like that? More to the point, could I invent that name? For reading we had all the riches of my father's one great extravagance—an overflowing library of some thousands of books. Books of all kinds in bookcases and piles and on tables everywhere in the house. Everybody read and read. And so did I. I remember reading Kipling and Stevenson and Dickens and Scott sooner than I was able to. And you could earn a quarter for reading any one of any number of hard books that my father thought anybody and everybody ought to read.

A few words about my father. For there were many things, more than the love of reading and writing and the gift of the ways and means to enjoy both, that he taught me by example and that at least precluded the possibility that most teachers could ever be as influential as he was. And there were other factors that, now that I am forced to think of it, must have led me to seek out coaches as teachers. Athletic teaching was the one great thing that he could not do for me. He had been an athlete and, I am told on good authority, a very good one, playing ice hockey and rowing in school and college. (Strange now to think that, among all the sports I tried and performed, those two never interested me much, and then only as a most casual spectator.) And he had led, for a time, a rugged physical life, dropping out of MIT to work in Utah as a copper miner. He wanted to be a mining engineer someday, but midway his money ran out; so he went to work in the mines out west, and he hoped to save enough money to go back to school. He had a slightly mangled left hand missing two full fingers, and bulky, powerful shoulder muscles, and a sinewy eighteen-inch collar size to show for his hard years as a miner. He had his membership in the United Mine Workers framed and on the wall, and in the attic there was a dusty old metal suitcase full of one kind and another of ore samples he had dug out himself. But he was crippled, which was what he called it, not being ever an advocate of euphemisms. Lame was more like it, though, for he had a bad leg and a limp left arm. Neither of which greatly impeded his apparent vigor and energy and, indeed, they were scarcely noticeable unless he tried to hurry, to run, or to leap up out of a chair. His lameness came in part from an injury and in part from a severe case of polio that had almost killed him. Now he could still swim—an awkward but powerful sidestroke—and he learned to play a pretty good game of tennis, hobbling it is true, but overpowering many good players with a hard backhand and a truly devastating and deadly forehand. He also had a quality possessed by one of his tennis heroes, Bitsy Grant. Somehow or other, in spite of all awkwardness and all disability, he would manage to return almost anything hit at him. He was hard to ace and you couldn't often get by him. When I was a boy, he was a ranked player, fairly high on the ladder of the local tennis club. Once or twice, over those years, he and a partner were number one, tops in doubles. None of which meant anything to me at the time. I was still young enough to be horribly ashamed of all that clumsy, awkward hobbling about. Young? I still wince with embarrassment to recall it, though now I have to believe that my youthful shame could never have equaled the embarrassment of his often younger and always more graceful opponents.

By the time I was born, he was a prominent, controversial, daring, and, in fact, feared lawyer, fearless himself. Together with his partner he drove the Ku Klux Klan, then a real political power, completely out of Kissimmee, Florida. And lived to enjoy the victory. Took on the big railroads— the ACL, the Florida East Coast, the Seaboard, and the Southern—and beat them again and again. Tried not one but any number of cases before the U.S. Supreme Court. Yet, at the same time and always, gave hours and hours of time, without stint, to those who were once called downtrodden. Especially to Negroes, who were more downtrodden than most anyone else. When black people came to see him at home, they came in by the front door and sat in the living room like anybody else. And nobody said a word about that or any of his other social eccentricities. Because most people, white and black, respected him and depended on him. With good reason. Once, in my presence (for, by his practice, all the family was included in anything that happened at our house), a deputation of lawyers from the various railroads offered him a retainer, much more money than he earned, in effect *not* to try any more cases against them. He didn't wait or consider his reply, though he surprised all of us by being polite. He thanked them for their flattering interest. He allowed as how it was a generous and tempting proposition.

"I would be almost a rich man," he said. "But what would I do for *fun?*"

And, laughing, he more shooed them than showed them out the door.

Naturally the thing I thought I needed and wanted most

of all was someone who could teach me hopping and skipping and jumping. Someone who could teach me how to run and how to throw a ball without the least hint of awkwardness.

Besides all that, there were some writers, real professional ones, on both sides of our family. On my mother's side was my grandfather's cousin Harry Stillwell Edwards. Whom I never met or even saw, but about whom I heard all kinds of family stories. One that stuck like a stickaburr, and I liked a lot, was how Edwards, who was then postmaster of Macon, Georgia, won a ten-thousand-dollar prize for his novel *Sons and Fathers*. Now that was a plenty of money, big money, even then when I heard about it. Child or not, I knew that much. But it was, as I would later learn, a huge sum, in the last years of the nineteenth century, to fall into the hands of a Southerner of most modest means. One who my grandfather always claimed owed him some modest sum of money. Didn't choose to repay it. Chose instead, as family story had it, to rent a whole Pullman car, fill it with family and friends, and take them all to New York City. Where the money was all spent in a week or ten days. Then back to Macon and life at the PO.

Nobody ever had to teach me anything about the potential joys and pleasures of the writer's life.

On the other side was an aunt, Helen Garrett, who wrote truly wonderful children's books and even won some national prizes for them, too. But she always wanted to be a novelist for adults, also, and somehow she never managed that.

Then there was Oliver H. P. Garrett, my father's surviving younger brother. (Another brother had been a mountain climber and a professional guide who vanished in a blizzard.) Oliver Garrett was a much-decorated soldier from the Great

War, a newspaper reporter for the old *New York Sun* who had interviewed Al Capone and, yes, Adolf Hitler, too, twice. First time on the occasion of the 1923 *Putsch,* from which Oliver Garrett predicted Hitler would recover and most likely come to some kind of dangerous power. Finally, in the early 1930s, with the advent of sound movies, Oliver went out, at the same time as a number of other good newspaper reporters, to Hollywood to be a screenwriter. And was, I learned much later, a very good one. Wrote dozens of good and bad and indifferent films. I have in front of me a copy of *Time* for 4 August 1930, which has a review of his movie *For the Defense* and a picture of him (page 25) and describes him as "said to be Manhattan's best-informed reporter on Police and criminal matters." Adding this little personal touch: "When Paramount began its policy of trying out newspapermen as scenario writers, he was one of the first reporters to become definitely successful in Hollywood. He is fond of driving a car fast, takes tennis lessons without noticeable improvement to his game, lives simply in a Beverly Hills bungalow with his son Peter, his wife Louise. Recently finding that he was going bald, he had all his hair cut off." He was one of the uncles, and a godfather, who sent extravagant and memorable presents on birthdays and Christmas; and once in a great while he would, suddenly and without any warning, appear for a brief visit. I recall a large man with a beret (first beret I had ever seen) and a long, shiny, yellow open car, with shiny spoked wheels and chrome superchargers. And colorful, short-sleeved shirts. And, usually, a beautiful wife or companion—there were several, of course. I remember that he could sing and play the guitar by a campfire on the beach. And most of what I know about World War I, I learned from him, from his stories of it.

Well, then. No lack of "role models" in those days. And early on, after I had announced that I intended to grow up to be a writer, I even managed to win a crucial approval. My grandfather on my mother's side, Colonel William Morrison Toomer, thoughtfully allowed that it would probably be all right for me to be a writer because "it is as good a way to be poor as any other." He added that I should not expect him to lend me any money, not after what cousin Harry did with all that prize money without bothering to pay Papa (as we called him) back whatever he owed him. Anyway, what could he say to me with sincerity and conviction when one of his own five sons, my uncle, was a professional golfer and another was a dancer? He was a little worried about what I would find to write about, concerned about my sheltered life and lack of experience. I must have been at most twelve years old when we talked. Well, when the captain and only other person on board was knocked cold and unconscious by the boom, my grandfather, about my age, had managed to sail a large schooner with a full load of cut timber successfully into the Charleston harbor. What he didn't stop to consider was that I already planned to use him and a lot of his experiences, whenever possible, to make up for the absence of my own.

In one sense he was right, though. Can you see that? What I needed to learn, what I had to be taught about before I could be myself at all and really write about any of it, was . . . life.

In school there were teachers, some very good ones as I remember, who were kind and were interested and who, I'm sure, tried to help me along at one time and another. But I was always what was politely known then as "an indifferent student," all the way through kindergarten, grammar school, junior high, and most of my high-school years. Those high-school years (and now we are coming close to the first of my coaches) were spent at the Sewanee Military Academy in Sewanee, Tennessee, that lonesome, isolated, beautiful, and changeless mountain village. The academy, or SMA as it was known then, is no longer with us. But in those days it was part, physically as well as bureaucratically, of the complex that formed the University of the South. Originally it had served as the preparatory school for the university, and even when I went there a very large number of the cadets aimed and planned to go to the university.

It is possible that I might as well have gone to Charleston and the Porter Military Academy there, which had been founded by Toomer Porter, a kinsman of my grandfather, and which my grandfather had attended in Reconstruction years. But I didn't want to go there, I recall, for just that reason; and, besides, there were other people from my hometown who attended Sewanee or were planning to go there. A whole group of us went together on the train. Overnight to Atlanta, where we changed trains. And where we urgently tried to buy clip-on black neckties, for none of us knew how to tie a tie. Then on to Cowan, Tennessee, raw and ramshackle (then as now) at the foot of the mountain. Then by a little train slowly through the woods and up the mountain to Sewanee.

Much has been written about the place of the military school in the scheme of Southern education. Calder Willingham in *End as a Man* (1947) and Pat Conroy in *The Lords of Discipline* (1980) have created successful novels out of their times at the Citadel. Ronald Reagan was one of the stars of the movie version of *Brother Rat*, all about VMI. And the subject has proved to be much alive and kicking, commercially viable to boot, as evidenced by a fine piece by Guy

Martin, an alumnus of the Baylor School in Chattanooga, appearing in the June 1985 issue—"The Soul of America: Golden Collector's Issue of 1985"—of *Esquire*. A basic point he makes is true enough—that within the context of the South, military school has always been considered more conventional than elsewhere and that, therefore, the military schools have not been wholly designed for and dominated by juvenile delinquents. True, we had our share of them, brutes sent off to be as far away from home as possible, to be, if possible, tamed and reformed without the stigma of reform school. And, as if to give these predators some function and sense of purpose, there was also a modest number of others, sissies in the persistent American term (remember Harry Truman calling Adlai Stevenson a sissy?), these latter sent off to be hardened and toughened, turned into "men." There were some of both types at Sewanee, but the majority were made of more ordinary stuff; though normalcy was tested to the quick by a schedule that began promptly, rain or shine, at 5:00 A.M. and ended with the bugling of taps, and lights out at Quintard Barracks, at 10:00 P.M., and all the time between (it seemed) spent in the daze of a dead run, running, marching, gulping meals—formations, classes, inspections, military science and tactics, all of it controlled by constant bugle calls. At one point, really until recently, I knew, by heart and by hard knocks, every single American military bugle call—from first call to taps and including such things as tattoo, call to quarters, guard mount, mail call, church call—the whole battalion of cadets marched, armed, flags flying and the band playing "Onward Christian Soldiers," to the chapel of the University of the South every Sunday morning regardless of creed or country of national origin. (There were no black students in white schools in the South in those days.) The handful of Catholics,

Jews, and, in the British terminology, Other Denominations were officially Episcopalians for the duration of their time at Sewanee. A rigorous schedule, then. And rigorous regulations, too. Only seniors, and then only as a special earned privilege, were allowed to possess radios, one per room. No point in it, anyway. There were about thirty minutes a day when the radio could be legally turned on. Everything you owned, folded in a precise manner and to the precise measured inch, had to fit neatly in a tin wall locker. No pennants, pictures, or decorations of any kind whatsoever. I remember that each cadet was allowed to possess one snapshot. Which was to be taped in its specific place and displayed on the wall locker. Some cadets put up a photo of a parent or parents. Some put up a (fully and decently clad; no bathing suits allowed by any means) picture of a girlfriend. There was quite a flap one year, as I recall, when a cadet who grew up and lived on a large central Florida cattle ranch taped up a picture of his favorite cow. This caused a great deal of controversy until it was finally decided, in favor of the cadet and the cow, by the superintendent, who was a brigadier general of the United States Army, in fact on active duty at the time. As were a fairly large percentage of the faculty. For these were the years at the beginning of World War II. Military training was very serious in any event, and especially at a few places in the country like Sewanee that still, in those days, could confer direct commissions on their outstanding graduates. Others went to West Point, VMI, and the Citadel and, I swear to you, reported back that they found these places relaxed and pleasant and easygoing in comparison with SMA.

One way or the other, it seemed in those days before the atomic bomb, we were all going to end up in the war. Some were already back with a limp or a hobble or a piece of metal plate in the head and the first one-thousand-yard stares most of us had ever seen. The army officers and NCOs on the faculty were not, outwardly and visibly, cripples at all, but clearly they were on limited service of one kind or another, most overage and easing into retirement with a final backwater tour of duty, a year or two in an odd and remote and more or less safe place. The regular, civilian faculty, who also wore uniforms and were identified by ranks, were, of course, more obviously disabled, unfit for the war that took away most of the able-bodied men. These teachers were 4-Fs, one and all, for one reason and another.

We were young and healthy, training as seriously as could be for a future of infantry combat. Wearing a variation on the traditional gray-and-black uniforms that, as I was to learn many years later while teaching as a visitor at VMI, were first introduced into this country and its military traditions by Colonel Crozet, the Napoleonic French officer who served as VMI's first superintendent. These were the uniforms of Napoleon's Young Guard, in which Crozet had served, and he brought them with him. Ever after that, VMI, the Citadel, West Point, and the mainstream military schools wore the gray wool trousers with the black stripe down the leg and variations on the choker-collared, tailcoated blouse that is called a *dyke* at VMI. Because it was the war, at SMA we dressed down, slightly, wearing for full dress a more modern blouse and, informally, a jacket resembling British battle dress or what was later called the Eisenhower jacket. No more high collars and white crossbelts. Indeed, for reasons I am not certain of except that everything was scarce in those years, we no longer wore white trousers in springtime, either. Often, for field training, we turned out in loose, baggy coveralls and old army canvas leggings. But we still had the old high-collared gray overcoat with its red-lined cape, and there were sabers and guidons at close-order drill. And drill had been simplified and streamlined for the vast citizen armies of World War II. I remember that the books and manuals we used were already out-of-date, no longer applicable in many large and small ways to the new ceremonies and the ways and means of dismounted drill. Sometime during those years the new field manual, *22-5, Drill and Ceremonies,* came in and became the bible for everything from full-dress parade to a single cadet, under arms, reporting to an officer indoors. (Under arms you did not remove your hat, or "cover," as it was called.) In those days, though, we still stacked arms by the numbers, linking rifles by threes, locked and twisted together with the now-vanished stacking swivels. And, in military courtesy, it was still the correct thing to address a superior commissioned officer not by his rank but by his duty, and only in the third person. Thus: "Does the company commander wish to move the company into the shade?"

So there we were, children in costumes but, in truth, not much younger than other children in costumes who were already fighting and dying in the Pacific and, soon, in North Africa, Sicily, Italy. We got V-mail from cadets who had graduated and gone on.

And there we were in the cool, fog-haunted, heavily timbered mountains of east Tennessee. We were lean and if not thriving, then enduring on skimpy institutional food, for which we had to furnish our ration cards and tickets like everybody else. There were moments in those days when most of us would have cheerfully fought to the death, or mighty close to it, for the sake of a hamburger or a piece of beefsteak. Still, the university had a first-class dairy herd (as did so many Southern schools and colleges in the depression and wartime);

and, in the absence of any other students except ourselves, a small V-12 Navy detachment, and a few 4-Fs and discharged casualties, we had all the milk and butter and cheese we could manage. Treats—a Coca-Cola, an ice-cream cone—were available at the university store, the "Soupy Store," about a half a mile or so from our barracks, which we were allowed to visit, providing we were not restricted to barracks for demerits or any other disciplinary or academic reason, on Sunday afternoons, following noon dinner and prior to parade formation, roughly from 1:30 to 3:30 P.M. Most of that time would be spent in line at the counter, listening to Jo Stafford records (over and over again, "Long Ago and Far Away," tunes like that on the handsome and primitive Seberg machine, or was it an early Wurlitzer?), hoping against hope to get served in time to drink or eat whatever it was that was available and that you could afford before the sound of the bugle blowing first call for parade sent everyone at a frantic, stomach-sloshing, breathless run back to barracks, to grab our rifles, our beautiful M1903 A3 Springfield rifles, and fall in for parade. . . .

Please. I am not complaining. Only describing. We were, with a precious few exceptions, too young, too ignorant and innocent, to complain about anything seriously. Growing up in the depression, coming of age in the war, we had no real luxuries to regret, nothing with which to compare, unfavorably, our busy and strictly limited little lives. Later I would find the army mostly an easy and pleasant ride compared with those years and would begin to wonder, as I do now, how I mustered up the energy and swagger to pass through an adolescence so aggravated by rigor and deprivation.

Girls? Odd you should ask. There were a few on the mountain, as I recall, altogether untouchable and, of course, utterly desirable. Otherwise there were formal dances once or twice a year. Some nice girls from some nice schools in Chattanooga and Nashville might be brought in by bus. Spick-and-span, barbered, scrubbed and brushed, shined and polished, we timidly met them at the gym and tried to fill out our dance cards (yes!) before the music began to play. I remember half-lights and the scattered reflections of a rotating ceiling globe. I remember how the whole gym seemed to seethe with the exotic odors of powder and perfume. I think the little band must have played "Body and Soul" over and over again. I remember a lot of standing and watching from the sidelines. There were some wise cadets, old-timers, who, given the choice, chose not to attend the dances. Went to the library instead. Or enjoyed the odd peace and quiet of an almost empty barracks. Without temptation and maybe without regret.

Where did athletics come in? What about the coaches?

Well now . . .

Athletics were everything. A way to escape the drudgery (and sometimes, for new cadets and younger ones, the danger) of the afternoons in the barracks or study hall. To be on a team meant an excused absence from some mundane and onerous chores. Best of all, it allowed for occasional forays off the mountain. A trip to play another school. Where there might be a chance to get a candy bar and a Coke, a Grapette and a Moonpie, at a bus stop or country store. A chance to see girls, maybe even, with luck, to speak to one. A chance in the "contact" sports to move beyond simple competition and to heap some measure of your own fury and frustration upon some stranger who was, most likely, seeking to do the same therapeutic thing to you.

Whom did we play against? It was, of course, the same

set of schools and places in all sports. But when I try to summon it up, I think of team sports. Of football most of all. It seems to me we played all the time, almost as much as we practiced. I suspect now that some of the games didn't really count. Were merely game scrimmages. Who knows? I do know that it was a long season, beginning in late summer and ending in boredom and bone-weariness sometime after Thanksgiving. We sometimes played a couple of games in the same week. On the one hand we played against east Tennessee high schools—Tullahoma, Murfreesboro, Lynchburg, etc., together with tiny country schools whose names I've long since forgotten. On the other we played against the other military schools: Baylor and McCallie in Chattanooga, both of which were bigger and generally better than we were, but for whom we had sneering contempt because their military lifestyle was casual (in our view), easygoing; Columbia Military Academy, which was, we believed, *all* athletics with no academics worth mentioning to interfere with sports, and where the players were bigger and more numerous than anywhere else; Tennessee Military Institute, which appeared to be *really* a reform school of some kind, wire fence around it, catwalks and searchlights and shabby khaki uniforms. And always our Episcopal neighbor, Saint Andrew's, with its monks and its poor boys who grew their own food. When we played them we had to play barefooted because they had no football shoes. They had a considerable advantage, tougher feet from playing barefoot all the time.

Equipment . . . there the war made itself known and felt. For sports like football, which called for lots of equipment, there was only old and worn and battle-weary stuff. Those were still the days of the high-topped, long-cleated football shoes that seemed to weigh about ten pounds apiece and made everyone except the most graceful and adroit seem to waddle about like ducks on dry land. Leather helmets without face masks. (Actually, the face mask was almost a decade away.) For people whose noses had been broken or whose teeth had been knocked out there were metallic half-masks called "bird cages," which no one would wear, no matter how urgently they needed to, because there were improbable horror stories of what would happen to you in a pileup if somebody on the other team grabbed your mask. There were thigh pads and hip pads and rib pads and shoulder pads, all of these hard leather and as heavy as can be. Often they seemed more trouble and danger than the injuries they were said to protect against. Football pants were heavy and bulky and baggy (except below the knee, where they ended) and made of something like canvas. Some high schools had enviable satinlike pants, but they tore easily and were deemed tacky. Our purple-and-white jerseys were of heavy wool—oh, long before the reasonable concept of the tear-away jersey. Sweat-soaked or rained on, they became a heavy burden to carry.

The truth is, we considered ourselves lucky, though, for we had the uniforms and equipment of the university to draw on to supplement our own. Theirs, like ours, were probably at least a decade old, but it was possible to tape and patch together something for each player. Most of the time. Shoes were such a problem—remember, too, that shoes were rationed in the war, and that included football shoes—that we might have been better off following the example of Saint Andrew's. Instead we did the best we could with what was at hand. I was not lonely or unusual in wearing three pairs of socks and stuffing the toes of my huge shoes with old newspapers.

If this was Real Life, if this was all the world that mattered and we were in it, then coaches were urgently important to us all. Trouble was that most of them didn't *teach* anything. They exhorted and denounced, praised and blamed, honored and ridiculed, but they seldom had any practical advice or real instruction for us. Those players who (somehow) already knew what to do were all right. And there were always a few athletes with great natural ability at this or that who figured out what to do by trial and error, intuition and inspiration. The rest of us ran about in shrill gangs, packs, and herds, desperately trying to make the elaborate diagrams of the coaches in our playbooks come to represent something real on the ground. The chaos of circles and *X*s on paper bore very little resemblance to anything happening in fact and particular. Nobody on either team ever seemed to be where he was supposed to be. But only the most cynical and worldly-wise among us concluded that the fault wasn't ours.

A word about formations.

It took the war (simplicity of systems for military players who could not afford the time to practice much) and the growth of the professional football business in the postwar years to simplify football. To reduce it, essentially, to uniform variations of the T formation. In the early 1940s there was a great variety of formations still in use. I recall the Notre Dame box (with and without a shifting backfield), the short punt, double-wing, and single-wing. And, of course, several kinds of T, which was, anyway, one of the oldest and earliest of formations.

Many things followed from this plethora of offensive systems. The most obvious was that, other things being equal, one *formation* might simply overpower another, particularly if there were an added element of surprise involved. To guard against surprise, scouting of opposing teams and any and all other forms of intelligence became important. I remember that we often knew, well in advance, the names and sizes and individual playing habits of opposing players. Sometimes this information was less than reassuring. It was not, for example, cheering news to discover that you would most likely be playing opposite someone several inches taller and fifty pounds heavier, someone whose play was characterized as extremely aggressive. Many teams did exactly what SMA did. They ran at least some plays from every one of the known offensive formations, what is now known as a "multiple offense," only more so. There were a number of coaching ideas behind this habit. One was that such flexibility allowed a team to switch from one offensive system to another, even during the course of a game, if the original offense was not moving the ball. It also allowed our team at least some familiarity with all the other formations, thus lessening the potential impact of surprise.

By the same token, there were certain inevitable results of building an offense depending on a complex variety of formations. One of these was that there was less time to spend on *defensive* formations. This was before the two-platoon system and unlimited substitution made for the kind of specialization you see in contemporary football. Players had to play both ways. As if by unwritten rule and certainly by accepted practice, defense was kept simple and brutal. Most teams most of the time stayed in a 6-2-2-1 defense. Sometimes shifting into a five-man line in a clear-cut passing situation. Or a seven-man line down at the goal line.

Another result was that there were so many plays to master, even against standard defenses, that nobody ever seemed to know them all. The starting lineup, the basic eleven players, had the advantage of specializing in only one position.

But behind them were the rest of us, the scrubs (as we were called then), who would probably be used very sparingly in any game, anyway, because of the complex and limited substitution rules. I remember that these rules kept changing every year, but they never made substitution easy. For at least a year or two, if a player left the game, he could not return until the next quarter. So starting players usually played on with minor injuries. But often injuries were not minor. Scrubs, therefore, had to be ready to play at more than one position just in case and if they hoped to play at all. I was merely typical in being ready to play wingback, quarterback, and both guards, left and right. In actual games I, and the others, might be asked to fill in at other positions.

The result of *all this* was—at least for all the players and, I would guess with confidence, an almost equal situation among the coaches—a great deal of dust and confusion on the playing field. Missed assignments, on both sides, were almost the rule rather than exception. Luck, pure dumb luck, became a much more crucial factor in every game. So did tricks and trickery. Fake substitution plays were common. Fake punts and field goals were frequent. The old Statue of Liberty play was always worth a try. I seem to recall rehearsing an elaborate fake-fumble play. All this nonsense only added to the general confusion and to the unpredictability of the games. Upsets were so commonplace they could hardly be called upsets. With so many variable and changing factors, even a state-of-the-art computer would be hard pressed to come up with any good clear patterns of probability.

Well, now, you are surely thinking. All of that must have been wonderful training for a life in the American literary world: hard knocks, massive confusion, fake punts, fake passes, and fake field goals, ceaseless trickery and treachery; and all of it depending on luck, on pure dumb luck.

And, once in a while, on coaching.

The coach who first reached me, taught me anything above and beyond the most basic fundamentals of the game, was Lieutenant Towles. I think. That is the name I remember. And the nickname, used by everyone except in front of him— "Lou-Two." Let us call him that, since that is what he was called.

Lou-Two was young and tall and lean, a splendid physical specimen. Except that he had somewhere lost an eye. Had one glass eye. And it was that, I imagine now, which kept him out of the war. I picture him now not in uniform, but in a neat sweat suit, long-legged and moving about the playing field in a sort of a lope, which was either imitated from or maybe borrowed by his two loping boxers, that always seemed to be at his heels. He was quick and just a little bit awkward, this latter I think because of being one-eyed. Some of the guys thought he was funny.

It was from Lou-Two that I began to learn some of the things that made a big difference in my life. I do not know if it was his intention to teach the things I learned. We sometimes learn what we want to quite beyond the intentions of pedagogy. (As Theodore Roethke put it—*We learn by going where we have to go.*) His concern at that time was teaching athletic skill. And that coincided with my interests. I had not the faintest notion that I might be learning things that would be transferable and could later be transformed into something altogether different—the art of writing. Athletic skill would grow, then fade later on with injuries, age, and change of interests. But attitudes and habits, together with something deeper than either, *rituals* really, would become so ingrained as to be part of my being.

At any rate I followed him into whatever sports he coached, season by season. He was one of several football coaches, an assistant, but he was head coach of boxing in winter and track in springtime. I had no particular natural ability at either of these sports. Swimming, which came easily, was my best sport. But I gave it up. To be coached by Lou-Two. I suppose I followed him because he had taken an interest in me and had encouraged me at a time when I was very eager but very easily discouraged.

(Here I should digress—digression being the essence of my style—and admit that deep within me, even to this day, the same child, of course, lives and bides his time. As a writer I am still easily discouraged and I still respond, with a kind of self-surrender, to encouragement and seeming interest. The difference is that now I know this about myself and am able to prepare to cope with it. I now know the name of the pain and have some rituals of damage control. I owe at least some of that difference—maturity?—to Lou-Two.)

His interest in and encouragement of myself and others, scrubs in life as well as athletics, now astonishes me more than it did then. By and large, coaches have their hands full just teaching and encouraging the few pupils and protégés who are already demonstrably talented and essential to the success of any given team. Which is why the great art or craft of contemporary coaching, at any level above the most elementary, is more a matter of careful and clever *recruiting* than anything else. They assemble teams of the gifted and experienced and they teach refinements only. Of course, this is one reason why, when you watch many college football games today, you will see that the main and often crucial mistakes are made in matters of fundamentals—missed blocks and tackles.

But in a little school like SMA, where teams were so often overmatched, it was probably good sense to try to make something out of the scrubs. They could, after all, make a difference as, inevitably, the basic team and its best backup players were worn down by attrition during the long season.

I am still speaking of football. Which was my chief goal. Like every other red-blooded Southern boy. It never occurred to me, then, to doubt that playing football was the most important thing a young man could do with himself. Except, maybe, to go to the war. From track I learned to run and then to run faster and faster. From boxing's hard school I learned any number of things, some of them more than physical. But chiefly at that age and stage I learned to cultivate a certain kind of aggressiveness, out of self-defense if nothing else. And I experienced a sharper, keener sense of contact. It soon dawned on me that for the most part and most of the time football was neither as tiring nor as dangerous as boxing. From boxing I began to learn to take punishment better, to know that it was coming, to bear it. But at the same time I was learning, with the pleasure of instant and palpable results, to dish out punishment. Learning by doing, by giving and taking, that others, even better athletes, did not enjoy receiving punishment any more than I did. I learned then that there was at least this much equality and that if I went after my opponents quickly, there were times when I could take command.

Shall I, may I say a word or two about pride and skill? Please understand that, at the age I am speaking from now, I am possessed, for better or worse, by very few illusions. I had even fewer at fifteen or sixteen. I was never a very good athlete. But, on the other hand, allowing that, I have been there and I have known the ups and downs, the feel of it all from head to toe. Which is (I do believe) much the same for all who have been there—regardless of their share of good luck or their degree of skill. I have won and lost races on hot cinder tracks and in cool swimming pools. In the ring (once and once only the selfsame ring—brass-corner posts, velvet-covered ropes, and bloodstained canvas—owned by a rich collector of such things, wherein Tunney beat Jack Dempsey the second time they went around) I have won and lost decisions, earned one draw, knocked out other young men, and, myself, have been battered and beaten to the sheer, dazed, vague, bloody, and bruised edges of unconsciousness. Never knocked out (yet), I am here to tell you, though. I have, yes, indeed, known those times when my mouth and tongue and jaws were too painfully swollen to open up wide enough for a teaspoon and when my bruised, puffy hands and sprained thumbs failed me at simple chores of buttons and shoelaces. Playing football in high school and college I experienced a few moments I can still honorably remember. I have run the ball and passed the ball. I have caught passes and punts. One time, once only, I ran back a kickoff for a grand total of twelve yards. I have tackled some well-known runners, including one Heisman Trophy winner. And one wonderful afternoon I somehow managed to fake out, block, and generally manhandle an All-American tackle. Who (when I think of it now) must have been just as astonished as I was when he kept on finding himself sitting firmly on the ground on his altogether ample ass.

And, oh sure, there are the ineradicable boo-boos and stupidities that will still wake me up in the middle of the night wincing with shame.

But from Lou-Two I was also learning other things that would prove useful. None of this learning was really verbal. It was a matter of feeling. It is only now, in the act of recalling it, that I am able to translate the experience into words and, thus, meaning. In those days I would have been severely challenged to be able to articulate even the most superficial aspects of my experience.

From him, first of all, I learned conditioning. Conditioning, then as now, only more so then, was more a mystery, more a matter of craft and secrets, than any kind of science. Faith and hope, I venture, had as much to do with being in shape as anything else. The same thing was true of the repair and healing of injuries in those days before there was anything called "sports medicine." Except for broken bones, the care of injuries was in the hands of trainers. Ours was the celebrated trainer of the University of the South, who, for the duration, had no teams to care for. He was an ancient black man named Willie Six. You went to his den at the university gym. After the basic amenities, you showed him your injury. He did things with heat and cold, with strong-scented and mysterious ointments and salves of his own making, and with deft massage. This healing was a vaguely religious experience. Sometimes, made whole as much by faith as treatment, I imagine, those who had hobbled in left cured and ready to play again.

Conditioning was mysterious like that. What you learned was that if you did certain things (and did without certain things) and performed certain rituals, your body would answer you by tiring more slowly and by recovering much more quickly from weariness, wear, and tear. You learned to know and to listen to your body. Since all this training was aimed toward the performance of a particular sport, its focus was less narcissistic than conditioning for its own sake or to improve appearance or health. The practical results of being in good shape, and, one hoped, better shape than others, showed up in performance. That in itself was a lesson of sorts that would carry over—that you could establish a relationship with the self of the body and the senses and could train it and teach it to work for you. And that you need not, indeed should not, be crazy or tyrannical in this matter. If you overtrained or mistreated your body, you lost ground.

What was happening, even during this period of concentration upon the body, was a kind of self-transcendence. In which, gradually and inexorably, the body, one's own, became in part something separate and distinct, an apparatus, a sensory instrument designed to do things and to feel things and to accomplish certain chores. It need not be a thing of beauty. It need only be able to perform, to the extent of its own learned limits, specific tasks. Inevitably one was, ideally, observing the body-self in action from a different angle and vantage point. An early lesson in point of view . . .

The larger value of this learning experience, however, was more complex and is even less easy to articulate. As I see it now it was a matter of learning one kind of concentration, of a kind that would be very useful to an artist. Concentrating on preparation, one could not afford to waste either time or energy worrying about anything beyond that. You were too busy preparing to worry about the game (or match or meet) until its moment arrived. And when that happened, it was pointless to worry about anything else, past or future, except the present experience. You learned to concentrate wholly on the moment at hand and to abandon yourself completely to it.

And *that* made sense out of all the chaos and confusion. Wholly given over to the present, you likewise limited focus to a tight, small area. To your own small space. To what you had to do. You became, for yourself, like a single lamp burning in a dark house. You learned to live in that light and space with only the most minimal regard for or awareness of all the rest of it going on all around you. You learned to play your part, early or late the same, and without regard for the score. Winning or losing didn't matter much.

The athletic advantages of this knowledge and concentration, particularly for an athlete who was making up for the absence of great natural skill, were obvious and considerable. Concentration alone gave you an edge and advantage over many of your opponents, even your betters, who could not isolate themselves to that degree. For example, in football if they were ahead (or behind) by several touchdowns, if the game itself seemed to have been settled, they tended to slack off, to ease off a little, certainly to relax their own concentration. It was then that your own unwavering concentration and your own indifference to the larger point of view paid off. At the very least you could deal out surprise and discomfort to your opponents.

But it was more than that. Do you see? The ritual of physical concentration, of acute engagement in a small space while disregarding all the clamor and demands of the larger world, was the best possible lesson in precisely the kind of selfish intensity needed to create and to finish a poem, a story, or a novel. This alone mattered, while all the world going on, with and without you, did not.

What I am saying is that in learning how to teach things to my own body and how to use myself to advantage I was learning something deep beyond words about the nature of inspiration and of intuition.

I was learning about the beginning of what is called, poorly, for lack of a better term, the creative process. I was learning this, first in muscle, blood, and bone, not from literature and not from teachers of literature or the arts or the natural sciences, but from coaches, in particular this one coach who paid me enough attention to influence me to teach some things to myself. I was (appropriately for a military school, I suppose) learning about art and life through the abstraction of athletics in much the same way that a soldier is, to an extent, prepared for war by endless parade-ground drill. His body must learn to be a soldier before heart, mind, and spirit can.

Lou-Two, perhaps without realizing or intending it, initiated me. It would be another man, a better athlete and a better coach, who would teach me most and point me toward the art and craft I have given my grown-up life to. But I could not have gained or learned anything from the second man, the next coach and teacher, if I had not just come under the benign if shadowy (for there is so much I cannot remember) influence of the first man.

A final track season; graduation; and I went my way, having so much by then absorbed what he had to teach that I took it all for granted without any special gratitude toward Lieutenant Towles or any special memory of him until now. I remember the two boxer dogs first. I fill in the man loping between them.

The next man had a certain fame. He was Joseph Brown, professor of art and boxing coach at Princeton University.

With Joe Brown I now encountered an artist, a sculptor, and a coach who had once been a great athlete. Never defeated as a professional fighter. And *just* missed being a world champion. Missed because he lost an eye in an accident while training for a championship fight. (Yes, oddly, he, like Lou-Two, was one-eyed.) As a coach, pure and simple, he had much to teach me. Or, better, there was much to learn from him. For one thing, he was able to show me that there were things, particularly habits derived not from poor coaching but from experience, that it was already too late to unlearn. Things I would have to live with. There were things, beginning with my basic stance as a fighter, that were "wrong" and less than wholly efficient and effective. I fought out of a kind of side-ways stance that allowed for a good sharp left jab and even a left hook and was an effective defensive stance, but limited the use of my right hand except in very close. He taught me how to analyze that stance (and other habits) and how, rather than discarding it and disregarding all the experience that had gone into forming it, to modify it slightly so as to take best advantage of its strengths and at the same time to com-pensate for its more obvious weaknesses. Compensation, that's what he showed me. How to compensate for what is and what isn't. Compensation for injury, compensation for inher-ent physical defect or bad habits.

What was happening, then, was the introduction of mind, of *thinking,* into a complex process that had been, until then, all intuition and inspiration, all ritual and mystery. He did not seek to eliminate these things, but he added another di-mension to them.

The practical values were immediate. For instance, I soon discovered that I was in far better physical condition than I had known. Learned that professional fighters planning on ten-round fights did not spend any more time than I was spending in the gym or doing roadwork. Why, then, was I completely worn out, exhausted, after three rounds? Because I was . . . not using my head. Thinking, being aware of what was happening as it was happening, was in fact relaxing. With thought you could not so much coast as control your expense of energy. Which did not mean that you spent any less of yourself. It became, though, a question of how and when you spent your energy. The ideal was to expend exactly what you had, to be exactly on Empty at the moment a given round (or the whole fight) ended.

This required a deeper, more objective consciousness of self. It also demanded a greater awareness of what was happening outside and around yourself. Football, at least serious football, was limited after my freshman year because of a serious knee injury. But, even so, I began, thanks to Joe Brown and the introduction of thinking into performance, to be aware of the wholeness of the game, of other things going on even as I was doing what I was supposed to do. With mind came choice. Vision was joined and fulfilled by revision.

From Joe Brown, both by teaching and example (he was still, close up, the best fighter I had ever seen), I began to learn the habits of professionalism, the kind of professionalism that would be demanded of me as an artist. Never mind "good" artist or "bad" artist. I even learned, through the habits of this kind of professionalism and the experience of trying and testing myself and my habits against others who also knew what they were doing, that nobody else, except maybe a critic-coach like Joe Brown who knew what was happening at all levels of his being, could honestly judge and evaluate your performance. I learned to recognize that the audience, even the more or less knowledgeable audience, never really knew what was going on. Nor should they be expected to. One soon had to pass beyond the stage of contempt for the ignorant audience and to recognize that their illusions did not make them contemptible.

I learned that in the end you alone can know and judge your own performance, that finally even the one wonderful coach-critic is expendable. He can solve a practical problem for you, a problem of craft, but he cannot and should not meddle with the mystery of it.

I learned something, then, about the brotherhood of fighters. People go into this brutal and often self-destructive activity for a rich variety of motivations, most of them bitterly
antisocial and verging on the psychotic. Most of the fighters I
knew of were wounded people who felt a deep, powerful
urge to wound others at real risk to themselves. In the beginning . . . What happened was that in almost every case, there
was so much self-discipline required and craft involved, so
much else besides one's original motivations to concentrate
on, that these motivations became at least cloudy and vague
and were often forgotten, lost completely. Many good and
experienced fighters (as has often been noticed) become gentle
and kind people. Maybe not "good" people. But they have
the habit of leaving all their fight in the ring. And even there,
in the ring, it is dangerous to invoke too much anger. It can
be a stimulant but is very expensive of energy. It is imprac-
tical to get mad most of the time.

Let me put it another way. In anecdote. All through my
youth I admired many fighters. Especially Joe Louis. One of
the many things I found admirable was that most of his moves
(most of his craft) were so subtle as to be lost on all but the
most knowledgeable fans. Once, in those days, I rode the Silver Meteor from New York to Florida, together with a young
heavyweight who had just that week fought a ten-round exhibition bout against Joe Louis. I remember (still a fan and
an amateur at heart) being amazed that this young fighter
was not overawed. He had great respect, of course, and some
awe. But even though he had been "carried," he had stood in
there and traded licks with the great man.

"You know what really surprised me?" the fighter said.
"His left jab. He has a very strong, fast left jab. It's his best
punch, really."

Since then I have studied the films and I think that is true. Louis's jab was so good that it caused pinwheels and cobwebs in his opponents' heads long before he got around to the right-hand punches that put them away.

(Try to imagine that kind of professionalism in literature. Something like: "That Hemingway, he can do a fish story about as well as anybody around.")

From Joe Brown I also learned something of the permissible vanity of the professional. Joe had long since outgrown any of the false and foolish pride of the athlete. But he knew himself well enough to know that some of the pride was earned and all right. Once in a great while he would go to the fights in New York at Madison Square Garden or Saint Nick's. If he went, he would be recognized, starting in the lobby with the old guys walking on their heels who sold programs. And the ushers. Before the main fight he would be introduced from the ring. He liked that moment even when it embarrassed him. It was a homecoming. He wrote a fine short story about it called, as I remember, "And You Hear Your Name." It was a good and true story about pride and mixed feelings.

Joe Brown was an artist and he was as articulate about his art as he was about his sport. He could talk about it, though always simply and plainly. For those who were tuned in to his kind of talk it was valuable. R. P. Blackmur, for example, used to discuss literary matters and matters of aesthetics with Joe. It was from Joe, Blackmur said, that he got one of his best-known titles—*Language as Gesture*. Which was a reversal of something I myself had heard Joe say: that in sculpture gesture was his language.

Many of his athletes also went, one night a week, to his sculpture class. It was, in those days before coeducation came to Princeton, always a Life class. The only place you could be sure to see a naked woman on the campus. A powerful inducement. We managed to learn a little about modeling clay and about the craft of hand and eye. For most of us what we learned was that we would never, ever be sculptors even if we wanted to. But, hand and eye, we learned some things that would carry over, despite a lack of natural talent.

Some of the intellectual lessons Joe Brown taught were brutally simple. In boxing, for example, he was fond of reminding his guys that to win in boxing you had to hit the other guy. To hit the other guy you had to move in close enough for him to hit you. No other way. One of the immutable lessons of boxing was that there was no free ride. No free lunch. To succeed you had to be at risk. You had to choose to be at risk. That choice was the chief act of will and courage. After that you might win or lose, on the basis of luck or skill, but the choice itself was all that mattered.

Or a matter of sculpture. Teaching something of the same sort of lesson. At one stage Joe was making a lot of interesting pieces for children's playgrounds. This in response to some Swedish things that were being put up in New Jersey and that, in Joe's view, while aesthetically interesting, had nothing special to do with *play*. He said a piece for a playground should be something you could play on and with. One of his pieces, I remember, was a kind of an abstract whale shape. High "tail" in the air and a slide from the "tail" through the inside of the "body" and out of the "mouth." It was tricky to get to the top of the "tail." There was no one and easy way to climb there. Many different ways as possibilities. Some of them a *little* bit risky. You could fall down. So? You can fall out of a tree, too, or off a fence. Falling down is part of growing up. But worth the risk. Once at the top of the "tail" there was the wonderful, steep S-shaped slide waiting. Only, right in the middle it leveled off. The experience of the slide was briefly interrupted.

Why?

"I want these kids to learn the truth," he said. "You can have a great slide, a great experience. But to do it all the way you've got to get up off your ass and contribute at least two steps of your own."

My first lesson in . . . *meaning in Art*.

As I am thinking about these things and writing about my thoughts, so much has changed. My father has been dead for many years. Lieutenant Towles disappeared from my life, and when I first wrote and published a version of this essay, I had no idea where he might be, even if he was alive or dead. I had not seen him again or heard from or about him since graduation day at SMA. But the world is always stranger than I imagine it to be, and after I published a version of this piece (and somebody read it and then showed it to him) I did hear from Towles, who was and is, it seems, alive and well and retired in Mississippi. Who wished me well and corrected an error in this piece. For the record, he did not have two dogs, only one very large one. And as I write this, I have news that Joe Brown died recently in Princeton. Thirty-five years and more have passed since he was my coach and teacher. And likewise the half child, myself, who came to him to try to learn and to improve his boxing skills, is long gone also, even though, by being alive, I can still carry the memory of him, that child, and thus, also, of Joe Brown. I can summon up the sweat and stink of that gym. Pure joy of it when things went well. Pain when they did not.

There were other teachers at other times, earlier and later, to be sure. Some who were much help. But none who changed my life so greatly as my two one-eyed coaches. No others whose influence has lasted so long, of whom I think often and against whose tenets and examples, even now, I test myself.

Ironically, I tend to dismiss most comparisons of athletics to art and to "the creative process." But only because, I think, so much that is claimed for both is untrue. But I have come to believe—indeed I have to believe it insofar as I believe in the validity and efficacy of art—that what comes to us first and foremost through the body, as a sensuous affective experience, is taken and transformed by mind and self into a thing of the spirit. Which is to say that what the body learns and is taught is of great significance at least until the last light of the body fails.

A Shepherd's
Adventure

1.

Once upon a time.

Once upon a time, in our family, we told each other stories. Begged, borrowed, stole them, ransacked the literature, the folklore and fairy tales of the past. And, worse come to worst, we had to make them up out of our own heads, out of whole cloth (as they say), seeking always the secret of creating a silk purse out of a sow's ear. Trying to learn the art and craft of Rumpelstiltskin (don't forget that name or we're in big trouble around here), how to turn dirty straw into pure gold.

Can it be done? Who knows? What we do know is that for a time we can believe in them, do believe in them, both the teller and the tale, for at least the time of the telling.

And—even though we have told and passed on stories to each other at all times, anytime—still some times of our lives, and of the turning wheel of seasons whose revolutions (yes) make up a year, may not be better or more propitious for tale-telling than others, but are certainly more magical. Christmas is like that, magic for many of us, one way and another. A time, as the calendar year comes toward its ending, for beginnings (where end and beginning meet and embrace), for wishing and hoping, for believing and wishing to believe. For remembering.

I remember that I once wrote a short poem about all that and some other things; wrote and published it about the time, almost thirty years ago now, that I had first moved to Charlottesville, Virginia, with my family, to teach English at the university. I think that I wrote it during that fall—it would be 1962—and sent it out on a Christmas card that year.

It was called "The Magi" and here it is, many Christmases later:

The Magi
First they were stiff and gaudy,
three painted wooden figures on a table,
bowing in a stable without any walls
among bland clay beasts and shepherds
who huddled where my mother always put them
in a sweet ring around the Holy Child.
At that season and by candlelight

it was easy for a child to believe in them.
Later I became one. I brought gold,
ascended a platform in the Parish House,
and muffed my lines, but left my gift
beside the cheap doll in its cradle,
knelt in my fancy costume trying to look wise
while the other two (my friends and rivals
for the girl who was chosen to be Mary)
never faltered with frankincense and myrrh.

Now that was a long time ago.
And now I know them for what they were,
moving across vague spaces on their camels,
visionaries, madmen, poor creatures possessed
by some slight deviation of the stars.
I know their gifts were shabby and symbolic.
Their wisdom was a thing of waking dreams.
Their robes were ragged and their breath was bad.

Still, I would dream them back.
Let them be wooden and absurd again
in all the painted glory that a child
could love. Let me be one of them.
Let me step forward once more awkwardly
and stammer and choke on a prepared speech.
Let me bring gold again and kneel
foolish and adoring in the dirty straw.

But all that, all of the above, is just to set the mood and
tone for what follows. More important than any formal printed
poems and stories, Christmas cards, or whatever, were the
tales we told each other in those days. Days not *before* television—for, in our innocence, we still loved our snowy little
black-and-white set with its corny programs and commer-
cials. Not before television arrived, then, but before that me-
dium was allowed to triumph over our better judgment and
pollute the spiritual atmosphere, perhaps beyond any repair.
But never mind. We still told each other stories, just as our
ancestors had in their caves in days beyond remembering. By
the fireplace in our house on Winston Road. Myself and my
wife and the three children, who were all in Venable School
in those days, and usually some grandparents or maybe rela-

tives from Richmond. Tales told on demand for the children and for their sake, close by the dance and sway of light and shadow coming from the fireplace and the sweet mixed odors of fat lightwood and slow-burning hardwood. Outside, it seems to me in the world of memory (and I can remember it as I please, can't I, so long as I am not indifferent to the facts, for memory is another magic form of tale telling, while the power and glory to remember last); outside there will be the soft, muting covering of the year's first big snowfall. It has been blowing and gusting all day long, an air freighted with swarms of snowflakes. But now the wind has gone calm and the world of our neighborhood is very quiet. The trees are ghostly, their limbs holding a huge white burden. Nothing is moving on the streets hereabouts and nothing will be, either, unless there is some trouble or emergency. At first light, when new light glints and glitters off the fresh snow, these three small children will join the others sailing down the steep hill of Winston on their sleds; or taking the breathless dive and S-turn of Fendall down, in a whoosh and rush, into Sally Mead's "gulch" (where she will have arranged a version of the Winter Olympics); or maybe later the long and lazy, call it stately, descent of Wayside Place.

The thoughts of the children are all about tomorrow. Perhaps it is even Christmas Eve—let us here stipulate that it is, adding intensity to their anticipation.

So there we are, there we were once, then, grouped about the fireplace, Christmas stockings hung in place on the mantel, children sipping sweet cocoa, grandparents enjoying some fresh, thick eggnog, Daddy (in those young days for sure) indulging, without a hint of inhibition, in a glass of darkly amber-colored bourbon and branch. Just the least splash of water, thank you kindly.

We have been telling stories. It comes to be my turn. And I have already told them all, all that I know of, anyway, borrowing and stealing shamelessly and without the least hint of attribution, offering my own versions and revisions, this year and for years gone by, emptying my Santa Claus sack of Christmas literature, everything I can remember from the wonderful slapstick of *The Second Shepherd's Play* (in my version written for performance by the Three Stooges, among others), on up through the spooky dreams and happy ending of old Scrooge and even a down-home plagiarism of Dylan Thomas. Never ever, I can promise you, not even encouraged by torture, to tell them the secular-commercial-sappy story of "Rudolph, the Red-Nosed Reindeer."

Anyway, I have somehow told them everything I know of, and so I will now be forced to *make up something* on my own. Sort of. I make a mild, perfunctory try to pass it on to someone else, knowing I won't and can't succeed. And I don't escape. I wing it.

I take a long cold/warm swallow of bourbon and branch, hoping the fumes and essence of the corn ("There's a lot of nourishment in an acre of corn," William Faulkner used to say) will awaken and attract the attention of the vagrant Muse. And so begin:

2.

How, once upon a time, there was a young shepherd boy . . .

What was his name?

Why, his name was Jedediah. Which is a Hebrew name meaning "God is my friend."

(I knew they would ask that; they always do; so I had

prepared a few names from the given names in the dictionary.)

Jedediah was called Jed for short, even in those days. Because *Jedediah* is a mouthful now and was a mouthful then. And the only people who ever called him by his long and full name were his mother and his father when they had some reason for annoyance or anger.

"Jedediah!" one of them would holler in a loud voice he could hear all the way from the cluster of tents where they lived to where he and other children were playing. "Jedediah!"

And his heart would flip-flop and his stomach would growl. The others would wink and make faces at him, enjoying his acute discomfort as he turned and, head hanging down, walked slowly back toward his tent and what was sure to be some kind of trouble. There was a lot of trouble, not always, but often enough.

Now, Jed was not a bad boy, really, and his parents and his brothers and sisters, younger and older, were not mean or cruel to him. At heart, Jed's trouble was very simple. He had a very active imagination. He could imagine all kinds of things happening, some of them pretty unusual. And sometimes these imaginary things, which came to him first in dreams or daydreams, were just as real to him as a rock he might really stub his toes on or trip over.

Because these imaginary things seemed real to him, he could be very convincing to other people. He seemed to be sincere and without much guile and they believed whatever he told them until it was proved to be completely false. Then, being mostly unimaginative people, or, to put it more accurately (for everyone has the gift of imagination to one degree or another), being people who did not trust their own imaginations anymore, they thought imagination was a child-ish and silly thing; so after they had been fooled a few times by young Jed—sometimes on purpose, as he would admit, for he liked to see their eyebrows go up like flapping wings and their mouths pop open and their skins turn pale and sweaty when he told them something really scary and won-derful—then they would not believe anything he said.

And some of the people complained to his parents that he was a bad influence on their children and was causing them to have nightmares or, sometimes, to copy him and make up outlandish stories that they called *lies*.

"Jedediah is a liar," they said.

"No," his mother said. "He tells the truth, most of the time, anyway. It's just that what is true for him isn't exactly the same as what is true for you and me. Do you under-stand?"

"I'm afraid not," they would say.

"Listen," she would go on. "Haven't you ever had a dream that was so real to you that, at least for a while after you woke up, you believed it had really happened to you?"

"Sure," they would say. "Everyone has that experience. But nevertheless, dreams are dreams. They are not really real."

"They're real to him. Jed is a dreamer. He is dreaming all the time."

"Well, be that as it may," they would say, "you should keep him away from the other children."

"Surely you don't mean that," she would say. "If he has to be alone all the time, to play by himself, he will just get deeper and deeper into dreaming things."

Then they would shrug. What else could they do? What could they say? So they would shrug their disapproval and turn their backs and walk away.

And she, his mother, would ponder these things in her heart and feel sad for her son. She was sorry that they misunderstood him. She believed that his imagination, like everyone else's, was the gift of God. She liked to think that God had given her son Jed a very good and active imagination for some purpose. Some purpose that she didn't know and couldn't, yes, imagine herself. But whatever it was would come to pass in the fullness of time and would be wonderfully clear when it happened.

"You're dreaming," her husband, Jed's father, said. "You sound just like him. The boy is just lazy and thinks too much. He needs to be kept busy. Idle hands are the devil's workshop. He needs to go to work."

All right. You want to know when and where. Well, this story took place a long, long time ago in what is now Israel. And these people were shepherds, nomads, really, for in that dry and desolate country they had to move about looking for places where their sheep could graze. They all lived in big tents (and, I know, I know, that might be fun for us, too, for a while anyway); and they didn't have to go to school. But they did have to go to work while they were still very young, your age, and work hard and long hours just like grown-ups.

Jed's father decided—and he was the absolute boss in that family—that Jed's mother was spoiling the boy and that Jed was going to get worse instead of better unless he learned more about real life and real things. So, even though Jed was still too young, his father took Jed with him and the other grown men and the older boys when they took the sheep to graze far from the camp.

And for a while he was so busy, learning all the things that a shepherd has to know and look out for, that he didn't have much time for dreaming and tall tales. But soon he felt at ease with his tasks and chores and he had more and more time on his hands while he watched over the herd of sheep. Soon he was daydreaming and imagining things just like before.

And he really did believe that he saw a great, big, huge wolf, twice as big as any dog he had ever seen or imagined, maybe as big as a lion would be, that came howling and snarling out of a cave in the rocks, huge teeth glittering in the sunlight like knife blades. And he ran for his life and called, "Wolf! Wolf!" to where the other shepherds were. And they all came running to kill the wolf or at least to chase it away.

Which they didn't have to do. Because when they got there, there wasn't any wolf. Just the woolly sheep quietly grazing as if nothing had happened. And that was the truth. Nothing had happened. There was no wolf and there never had been any real wolf. There wasn't even a cave in the rocks.

Now, I know. You think you have heard this story before. You think it's about the boy who cried wolf. But it isn't. Not exactly. I mean, you're right. This boy, Jed, did cry "Wolf! Wolf!" But he isn't the same boy and it isn't exactly the same story. Lots of people cry "Wolf!" and sometimes there even is a wolf and he eats them up.

Now then. Jed's father was very embarrassed and disappointed. And he was angry too, partly because when they all got there and Jed realized that it had been an *imaginary* wolf that had caused all this excitement, he started laughing. He laughed and laughed. He kept laughing until his father took a switch and spanked him, in front of all the others, until he cried. He added to Jed's punishment by making him go without any supper and stay up all night and watch the sheep while the others curled up and slept close to a big fire in their little camp.

Jed could prove himself and make up for his dumb joke by staying up all night, all by himself, well away from the fire and the camp.

It was a very cold and clear night. The stars were bright and seemed near. He thought he could throw a rock and hit the low stars. He kept moving to keep from getting too cold and to keep from falling asleep. He thought that as long as he could keep moving around he would be all right. He was cold and sleepy and hungry and a little bit afraid. Partly because he knew the story of the boy who cried wolf also. People had told Jed that story lots of times. And he was afraid that the next time a wolf appeared it would not be an imaginary one.

Nevertheless, in spite of his good intentions, he stopped and leaned on his shepherd's crook and closed his heavy eyes, just for a minute, mind you, to rest them, and dozed off.

When he woke up something was terribly wrong. The whole field was as brightly lit as if it had been on fire. It was aflame, but not hot like a fire. Out of the blazing of fire and light came the sounds of music playing and then came into view a shining giant, all aglitter with light and silver and gold and a rainbow of jewels and precious stones.

"Surely it is the king from Jerusalem," Jed thought as he knelt down politely. "The king has come to punish me for imagining things."

But as this blazing, light-thrilled creature came closer, Jed saw that it was not a king and not a man at all, but something like a man, a beautiful and perfect man, with huge and shining wings.

Jed thought his imagination was playing a great and terrible trick on him and that whatever happened would be the worst thing that had ever happened to him. He was all of a sudden deeply, desperately afraid.

"Fear not!" said the shining being, as if he could read Jed's mind. Which he could. "For behold, I bring you good tidings of great joy, which shall be to all the people."

And the shining one told him to hurry and wake up all the shepherds and tell them the good news. That in the city of David, called Bethlehem, was born this day a Savior, which is Christ the Lord.

"I will do what you say," Jed said. "But they'll never believe me."

"Go," said the angel. "Hurry!"

And Jed left the herd and ran all the way back to the camp, where the shepherds were snoring and the fire was dying. He had tears in his eyes and running down his cheeks, partly because he knew what would happen to him when he woke the shepherds up, but also because he had just seen the most beautiful and wonderful thing he could possibly imagine, almost beyond all believing and imagining, and he felt sorry for the others, who had not been chosen to witness this thing.

He woke them up and they stood up grumbling and growling. He told them, as best he could, what he had seen and what he was supposed to tell them. They stood there around him, silent and furious, until his father spoke to him.

"Jedediah," he said sadly, softly, "I understand. You are possessed by a demon or a devil. You can never learn. You will never be like other people."

Just then the whole world, earth and sky, lit up as if with summer lightning, but much brighter than that, with an almost blinding light. And not one angel, but a multitude of them, filled the air with their great wings. And the same one who had come to him now came to them all where they one and all knelt in fear and trembling. He told them his same message, just as Jed had repeated it.

And then all together, in a chorus, the angels were singing: "Glory to God in the highest, and on earth peace, goodwill toward men."

When the angels had vanished and the night and the stars returned around them, the shepherds rose to their feet and looked at each other.

"Let us go now unto Bethlehem," Jed's father said. "Let us go and see this thing which is come to pass, which the Lord hath made known unto us."

And they hurried off in the darkness in the direction of Bethlehem.

Jed started to follow them, then realized that if he went, too, there would be no one left to watch over the sheep. So he stayed behind, wide awake now. His father would tell him all about it when they came back. Besides, he could imagine it all, anyway—the manger, the animals, the father and mother and the holy Child. He could imagine it and it was just as real as if he had been there with the others.

And now, children, it's time for you to go up to your real beds and really go to sleep and dream about Christmas morning. Which will be here, really and truly, very soon.

Good night and sleep tight. . . .

4.

Somewhere or other the great poet Yeats wrote these words, and I wrote them down, word for word, in my notebook: "I now can but share with a friend my thoughts and my emotions, and there is a continual discovery of difference, but in those days, before I had found myself, we could share adventures."

Now I am a grandfather. Now, after living and working all over the country, I live in Charlottesville again, a couple of blocks from where we lived then on Winston Road and told stories by the fire. And if I have not yet seen an angel on Wayside Place, I have sure enough seen a black bear, bigger than any football player, in our backyard a summer ago. And I believe (sometimes) that good angels brood over us and our lives, all the time, wishing us only well, wishing that our lives could be better than we can make them. Just as we wish that we could be there, too, with the shepherds and the wise men and the ghosts of those whom we have known and loved in life (so many, kinfolk and old friends, rest in peace) and always the bright angels of imagination, all of us kneeling together, once upon a time in that remembered stable, "foolish and adoring in the dirty straw."

A Wreath
for Garibaldi

The beginning was perfectly casual, offhand, pleasant. We were sitting on the terrazzo of a modern Roman apartment drinking coffee and thick, sweet, bile-colored Strega. It was an afternoon in late March; the air was fresh and cool, the spring sunlight rinsed and brilliant. The English lady, a poet and translator, was in the hammock and the rest of us sat around in wicker chairs—an artist, an Italian princess, another translator, an expatriate gentleman from Mobile, Alabama, who writes poems about monkeys. A usual crowd . . .

The talk was about politics. A pope had died, the new pope had been elected amid rumors and fears—*"Un Straniero per Il Papa?"* all the headlines read for a while—and errors: white smoke pouring out of the chimney of the Sistine Chapel on the very first ballot, inadvertently and incorrectly announcing the election of a new pope, because somebody had forgotten the straw to darken the smoke. The latest government had fallen. A coalition with more strength to the right (gossip had any number of known ex-Fascists among its members) had replaced it. The talk was of politics and, inevitably, the signs of the reawakening of fascism. Mussolini was being treated with nostalgia and kid gloves in a major picture magazine. Another magazine had been publishing a series about the war, showing how they (the Italians) had lost it by a series of "mistakes" and recounting moments of bravery and success wherever they could find them. There had been a television series on recent Italian history. Everybody had been waiting to see how they would manage to handle the whole big business of fascism and the war. It was disappointing. The producers treated the subject like scholars from a distant land, or maybe outer space, with careful, neutral disinterest.

making some headlines by dropping mice in tiny parachutes from the ceiling of a theater during an anti-Fascist comedy. There had been the "striptease incident" in a Trastévere trattoria when a Turkish girl took all her clothes off and did a belly dance. It was a very large private party, and most people missed that part of the show. More noticed the American movie star, one of the new sex symbols, who came with a buzz and hive of fairies (like Lady Brett?) and danced barefoot (like Ava Gardner?). In fact, the striptease never would have been an issue at all except that somebody took some photographs. The place was full of plainclothesmen who had come to protect the guests' jewels, but they didn't go into action until the next morning, when a tabloid appeared with the pictures of the belly dance. In no time the party was officially an orgy and there were lots of political implications and ramifications. It was the special kind of public prudery that interested the observer, though, the kind that had always been associated with the Fascist days. And there had been other signs and portents, like the regular toppling over and defacing of the bust of Lauro di Bosis near the Villa Lante on the Gianicolo.

Something was happening all right, slowly, it is true, but you could feel it. The Italians felt it. Little things. An Italian poet noticed the plainclothes policemen lounging around the area of Quirinale Palace, the first time since the war. At least they hadn't stepped up and asked to see his papers in the hated, flat, dialect mispronunciation of Mussolini's home district—*Documenti, per favore.* But—who knew?—that might be coming, too, one of these days. There were other Italians who still bore scars they had earned in police-station basements, resisting. They laughed and, true to national form and manners, never talked too long or solemnly on any subject at all, but some of them worried briefly out loud about short memories and ghosts.

We saw Giuseppe Berto at a party once in a while, tall, lean, nervous, and handsome, and, in my opinion, the best novelist of them all except Pavese. And Pavese was dead. Berto's *Sky Is Red* had been a small masterpiece and in its special way one of the best books to come out of the war. Now he was married to a young and beautiful girl, had a small son, and lived in an expensive apartment and worked for the movies. On his desk was a slowly accumulating treatment and script of *The Count of Monte Cristo.* On his bookshelves were some American novels, including Bellow's *Seize the Day,* that had been sent to him by American publishers. But he hadn't read them, and he wasn't especially interested in what the American writers were up to. He was very interested in Robert Musil's *Man Without Qualities.* So were a lot of other people. He was interested in Italo Svevo. He was slowly thinking his way into a new novel, a big one, one that many people had been waiting for. It was going to be hard going all the way for him because he hadn't written seriously for a good while, except for a few stories, and he was tired of the old method of *realismo* he had so successfully used in *Sky Is Red*. This one was going to be different. He had bought a little piece of property down along the coast of the hard country of Calabria that he knew so well. He was going to do one or two more films for quick cash and then chuck it all, leave Rome and its intellectual cliques and money-fed life, go back to Calabria.

Berto seemed worried, too. He knew all about fascism and had put it down in journal form in *War in a Black Shirt*. He knew all about the appeal of a black shirt and jackboots to a poor, southern peasant boy. He knew all about the infection and the fever, and, too, the sudden moment of realization when he saw for himself, threw up his hands, and quit, ending the war as a prisoner in Texas. Berto knew all about fascism. So did his friend, the young novelist Rimanelli. Rimanelli is tough and square-built and adventurous, says what he thinks. He had put it down in a war novel, *The Day of the Lion*. These people were not talking much about it, but you, a foreigner, sensed their apprehension and disappointment.

So there we were, talking around and about it. The English lady said she had to go to Vienna for a while. It was a pity, because she had planned to lay a wreath at the foot of the Garibaldi statue which towered over Rome in spectacular benediction from the high point of the Gianicolo. Around that statue in the green park where children play and lovers walk in twos and there is a glowing view of the whole city, in that park are the rows of marble busts of Garibaldi's fallen men, the ones who one day rushed out of the Porta San Pancrazio and, under fire all the way, up the long, straight, narrow lane, first to take, then later to lose, the high ground of the Villa Doria Pamphili. When they finally lost it, the French artillery moved in, and that was the end for Garibaldi, at least that time, on 30 April 1849. Once out of the gate Garibaldi's men had charged straight up the narrow lane. We had walked it many times and shivered, figuring what a fish barrel it had been for the French. Now the park is filled with marble busts and all the streets in the immediate area have the full and proper names of the men who fell there.

We were at a party once and heard an idealistic young European call that charge glorious. Our companion was a huge, plainspoken American sculptor who had been a sixteen-year-old rifleman all across France in 1944. He said it was stupid butchery to order men to make a charge like that, no matter who gave the order or what for.

"Oh, it would be butchery all right," the European said. "We would see it that way today. But it was glorious then. It was the last time in history anybody could do something gloriously like that."

I thought, Who is older now? Old World or New World?

The sculptor looked at him, bug-eyed and amazed. He had made an assault once with 180 men. It was a picked assault company. They went up against an SS unit of comparable size, over a little rise of ground across an open field. Object—a village crossroads. They made it and killed every last one of the Krauts, took the village on schedule. When it was over, eight of his company were still alive and all eight were wounded. The whole thing, from the moment when they climbed heavily off the trucks, spread out, and moved into position just behind the cover of that slight rise of ground and then jumped off, took maybe between twenty and thirty minutes. The sculptor looked at him, let the color drain out of his face, grinned, and looked down into his drink, a bad martini made with raw Italian gin.

"Bullshit," he said softly.

"Excuse me," the European said. "I am not familiar with the expression."

The apartment where we were talking that afternoon in March faced onto the street Garibaldi's men had charged up and along. Across the way from the apartment building is a ruined house, shot to hell that day in 1849 and left that way as a kind of memorial. There is a bronze wreath on the wall of that house. Like everything else in Rome, ruins and monuments alike, that house is lived in. I have seen diapers strung across the ruined roof.

The English lady really wanted to put a wreath on the Garibaldi monument on 30 April. She had her reasons for this. For one thing, there wasn't going to be any ceremony this year. There were a few reasons for that too. Garibaldi had been much taken up and exploited by the Communists nowadays. Therefore the government wanted no part of him. And then there were ecclesiastical matters, the matter of Garibaldi's anticlericalism. There was a new pope and the Vatican was making itself heard and felt those days. As it happens the English lady is a good Catholic herself, but of a more liberal political persuasion. Nothing was going to be done this year to celebrate Garibaldi's bold and unsuccessful defense of Rome. All that the English lady wanted to do was to walk up to the monument and lay a wreath at its base. This would show that somebody, even a foreigner living in Rome, cared. And then there were other things. Some of the marble busts in the park are of young Englishmen who fought and died for Garibaldi. She also mentioned leaving a little bunch of flowers at the bust of Lauro di Bosis.

It is hard for me to know how I really feel about Lauro di Bosis. I suffer from mixed feelings. He was a well-to-do, handsome, and sensitive young poet. His bust shows an intense, mustached, fine-featured face. He flew over Rome one day during the early days of Mussolini and scattered leaflets across the city, denouncing the Fascists. He was never heard of again. He is thought either to have been killed by the Fascists as soon as he landed or to have killed himself by flying out to sea and crashing his plane. He was, thus, an early and spectacular victim. And there is something so wonderfully romantic about it all. He really didn't know how to fly. He had crashed on takeoff once before. Gossip had it (for gossip is the soul of Rome) that a celebrated American dancer of the time had paid for both the planes. It was absurd and dramatic. It is remembered and has been commemorated by a bust in a park and a square in the city that was renamed Piazza Lauro di Bosis after the war. Most Romans, even some of the postmen, still know it by the old name.

Faced with a gesture like di Bosis's, I find usually that my sentiments are closer to those of my sculptor friend. The things that happened in police-station basements were dirty, grubby, and most often anonymous. No poetry, no airplanes, no famous dancers. That is how the real resistance goes on, and its strength is directly proportionate to the number of insignificant people who can let themselves be taken to pieces, piece by piece, without quitting too quickly. It is an ugly business and there are few, if any, wreaths for them. I keep thinking of a young woman I knew during the Occupation in Austria. She was from Prague. She had been picked up by the Russians, questioned in connection with some pamphlets, then sentenced to life imprisonment for espionage. She escaped, crawled through the usual mine fields, under the usual barbed wire, was shot at, swam a river, and was finally picked up in Linz. She showed us what had happened to her. No airplanes, no Nathan Hale statements. Just no simple spot, not even a dime-sized spot, on her whole body that wasn't bruised, bruise on top of bruise, from beatings. I understand very well about Lauro di Bosis and how his action is symbolic. The trouble is that, like many symbols, it doesn't seem to me a very realistic one.

The English lady wanted to pay tribute to Garibaldi and to Lauro di Bosis, but she wasn't going to be here to do it. Were any of us interested enough in the idea to do it for her, by proxy so to speak? There was a pretty thorough silence at that point. My spoon stirring coffee, banging against the side of the cup, sounded as loud as a bell. I thought, What the hell? Why not? And I said I would do it for her.

I had some reasons too. I admired the English lady. I hate embarrassing silences and have been known to make a fool out of myself just to prevent one. I also had and have feelings about Garibaldi. Like every Southerner I know of, I can't escape the romantic tradition of brave defeats, forlorn lost causes. Though Garibaldi's flight was mighty small shakes compared to Pickett's charge—which, like all Southerners, I tend to view in Miltonic terms, fallen angels, etc.—I associated the two. And to top it all I am often sentimental on purpose, trying to prove to myself that I am not afraid of sentiment. So much for all that.

The English lady was pleased and enthusiastic. She gave me the names of some people who would surely help pay for the flowers and might even march up to the monument with me. The idea of a march pleased her. Maybe twenty, thirty, fifty . . . Maybe I could call Rimanelli at the magazine *Rottosei,* where he worked. Then there would be pictures, it would be in the press. I stopped her there.

"I'll lay the wreath," I said. "But no Rimanelli, no press, no photographers. It isn't a stunt. As soon as you start mucking around with journalists, even good guys like Rimanelli, it all turns into a cheap stunt."

She was disappointed, but she could appreciate how I felt.

And that was that. The expatriate poet started telling a long, funny story about some German scholars—"Really, I mean this *really* happened"—who went down to the coast of East Africa somewhere near Somalia to study the habits of a group of crab-eating monkeys, the only crab-eating monkeys left in the whole world. These monkeys swam in shallow water, caught crabs, and ate them. So down went the German scholars with a lot of gear to study them. They lived a very hard, incredibly uncomfortable life for a year or so and collected all the data they needed. Then they came back to civilization and published a monograph. The only trouble was that the ink was hardly dry on the monograph before the monkeys, perverse and inexplicable creatures, stopped swimming entirely, stopped eating crabs for good and all, and began digging for clams.

Everybody laughed and our host poured out some more Strega.

Then it was almost the end of April. The English lady was in Vienna. I had been working on a novel, one about politics in Florida of all things, one that nobody north of the Mason–Dixon was to believe as probable (south of the line it was taken, erroneously too, as a *roman à clef*) and damn few people were going to buy. I hadn't seen anybody except my own family for a while. I couldn't get much interest or action out of the people who were supposed to help pay for the flowers. Some of them were getting kind of hard to get in touch with. I had a postcard from the English lady reminding

me of it all and wishing she could be there with me. I thought
a little more about Garibaldi, read about the battle in detail
in the library of the American Academy. Remembered Professor Buzzer Hall at Princeton and his annual show, the
passionate Garibaldi Lecture, the same one every year, that
drew enormous crowds, cheering students and half the Italians from Mercer County and Trenton. Hall could make you
want to put on a red shirt and go out and die. I had some
nostalgia about red shirts too. My grandfather had ridden
with Wade Hampton's Redshirts in Reconstruction days in
South Carolina.

I walked in the park of the Gianicolo many times. The
American Academy, where I worked, was on Via Angelo
Masina, and I had hunted for Masina, found his bust, and
found it defaced. Somebody had painted out *Angelo* and painted
in *Giulietta*.

I was going to do it, all right.

Then somebody stopped in my studio for a drink. He
said I ought to think about it; maybe it was against the law
or something. But how would I find out whether I was
breaking the law or not? By getting myself arrested? Then I
remembered I had a friend down at the embassy and I thought
I'd ask him to find out for me, even at the risk that he would
get very excited and patriotic. I called and we had a conversation that went about like this:

"Hello, John," I said. "Would you do me a favor?"

"What?"

"I'm going to put a wreath on the Garibaldi monument
on the thirtieth of April. Would you find out if I'll be breaking any law?"

"All right," he said. "Don't call me, I'll call you."

Not even in his tone was there the suggestion of a raised

eyebrow. Strictly routine. It would probably be the easiest thing in the world. Then he called back.

"Look," he said. "This may take a little time and doing. You sure you want to lay a wreath on the monument?"

"Well, I don't know. . . ."

"Do you or don't you? I mean, if you do, we'll fix it up. It's a little bit complicated, but if you want to do it, we can fix it."

I shrugged to myself. "Okay, see if you can do it."

I wasn't going to be able to hide behind the long skirts of the U.S. Government. This wasn't the timorous State Department I was always hearing about. He now acted as liaison and as a buffer between me and the Italian government. He, or his secretary, to be perfectly factual and to complicate things a little more, called me. There was a list of questions, some things they wanted to know before I got the permission. I would get the permission all right and it really didn't make much difference how I answered the questions, so long as I did not object to answering them in principle. She read the questions over the phone, completely matter-of-fact, and I dictated answers. There was quite a list, among them:

"Why are you laying a wreath on this monument?

"What special significance do you attribute to the thirtieth of April?

"Could there be any connection between the fact that the wreath is to be put there on the thirtieth of April and that the next day is the first of May—May Day?

"How many people do you anticipate will participate in this ceremony?

"Will they march? Will there be banners, flags, music, et cetera?"

And so on. The last question stopped me cold. I had also mentioned the bunch of flowers.

"Who is this Lauro di Bosis?"

I answered them all, each and every one. The secretary took down my answers, said she would relay them to Them and would call me back. A day or so went by before she called.

"It's all set," she said. "Go ahead and lay your wreath. They'll have police up there to protect you in case anything goes wrong. Just one thing, though: they're letting you do this with the full understanding that it doesn't mean anything."

"What?"

"They say it's all right because we all understand that it doesn't mean anything."

"Just a typical American stunt. No implications, some kind of a joke."

"That's the idea."

"Thanks a lot."

I was left with it in my lap then. If I put the wreath on the monument and flowers beneath the bust of Lauro di Bosis, it wouldn't mean a thing. If I did it, I was agreeing with that. They didn't care much about di Bosis anyway. "Who was he?" they had asked. I thought they were just testing or being ironic in the heavy-handed way of governments. They were not, it appeared. I had replied simply with the information that there was a bust of the poet di Bosis in the park. The secretary told me this was news to Them. Even if I did lay the wreath, it wasn't going to come close to fulfilling the intentions of the English lady. The hell with it. I would sleep on it and figure out what to do in the morning, which happened to be 30 April.

In the morning it was clear. The day was bright and warm and sunny. I walked over from my apartment to the Academy past the Villa Pamphili and along the route, in reverse, of Garibaldi's fallen soldiers. I passed by the English lady's apartment, the ruined house, the Porta San Pancrazio. Two horse policemen, mounted *carabinieri,* were in the shade of the great gate. A balloon man walked by, headed for the park in the Villa Sciarra, which is popular with children and where there is a wall fountain celebrated in one of the most beautiful poems written in our time. Americans in the area simply refer to it as Richard Wilbur's fountain. I watched the balloon man go along the wall and out of sight, followed by his improbably bright bouquet of balloons. I had a coffee and cognac at the Bar Gianicolo and made up my mind not to do it. I felt greatly relieved. I thought she would understand under the circumstances.

But, even so, it was a long, long day. The afternoon was slow. I couldn't make my work go, spent the whole time fiddling with a sentence or two. I went for a walk in the park. Children were riding in high-wheeled donkey carts. A few tourists were along the balustrade, looking at the vista of Rome. And there were indeed a few extra policemen in the area. I wondered what they thought they were looking for—some lone, crazy American burdened with a huge wreath—and what they would report when nothing happened, and who among Them would read such a report and how many, if any, desks it would pass over. I looked at Garibaldi. He wasn't troubled by anything. He was imperial and maybe a little too dignified to be wholly in character. He wasn't made for bronze. The traffic squalled around him, and behind him the dome of Saint Peter's hovered like a huge gas balloon, so light it seemed in the clear air, tugging on a string. If you went over to that side of the piazza you saw sheep grazing on a sloping hill beneath, with that dome dominating the whole sky. Once there had been a shepherd, too, with pipes, or, anyway, some kind of wind instrument.

I went on, took a look at Anita Garibaldi, another bronze equestrian, but this one all at a full gallop, wide open, a baby in the crook of one arm and a huge, long-barreled revolver in her other hand, which she was aiming behind her.

Diagonally across from Anita is the Villa Lante and the slender, lonely white bust of Lauro di Bosis. I went over and looked at him a while. Pale, passionate, yes glorious, and altogether of another time, the buzz of his badly flown airplane like the hum of a mosquito and of not much more importance when you think of a whole wide sky filled with the roar of great engines, the enormous bombs they dropped, thinking of my sculptor friend losing all his friends (and in war that's all that there is) as they came up over the slight rise in the ground and rushed the village across an open field. . . . He said there was a tank-destroyer captain with them. He had come along to see how it would go. He had been refused permission by Battalion to detach any of his idle tank destroyers to help the company out. He came just behind the assault, stepping over the bodies and weeping because just one tank destroyer could have taken the village and they never would have lost a man. Or thinking of all the brave anonymous men, *bravery* being a fancy term for doing what you have to and what has to be done, who fought back and died lonely, in police-station basements and back rooms, not only in Rome but in most of the cities of the civilized world. It was a forlorn, foolish, adolescent gesture. But it was a kind of beginning. If Mussolini was really a sensitive man, and history seems to indicate that he must have been (perhaps to his own dismay), then he heard death, however faintly, the flat sound of it—like a fly trapped in a room. I looked at Lauro di Bosis for a moment with some of the feelings usually attributed to young girls standing at the grave of Keats.

And that was the end of it.

Except for one thing, a curious thing. That same night I had a dream, a very simple, nonsymbolic dream. In the dream I had a modest bouquet of flowers and I set out to try to find the bust of Lauro di Bosis and leave the flowers there. I couldn't find it. I had a sense of desperation, the cold-sweat urgency of a real nightmare. And then I knew where it was and why I hadn't noticed it. There it was, covered, bank on bank, with a heaped jungle of flowers. It was buried under a mountain of flowers. In my dream I wept for shame. But I woke then and I laughed out loud and slept soundly after that.

Doing the Literary

At times sick unto death of myself
and the lies I tell myself, waking, walking,
sleeping, dreaming, lies that must choke
and gag me like a drunk man's vomit
until I lie (indeed) on the ground,
face the color of a bruise, arms and legs
kicking vain signals like a roach on its back,
I could crack my pen in two like a bone,
a thin bone, wishbone, meatless, chewed
down to the slick and bitter surface. . . .

—"Fig Leaves"

How to Do
the Literary

How this came about. Eight of us—Max Apple, Donald Barthelme, Doris Betts, William Gass, John Irving, Wright Morris, Lee Smith, and myself—were all invited to come to a kind of literary circus at the University of Alabama to talk, in one way and another, about the general subjects of voice and style. It was purposefully uncoordinated. Everybody came up with something different.

The stars of the show, the two who presented (separately) evening performances from the stage of a large theater, were Wright Morris and John Irving. Irving was at the peak of his commercial success and high public visibility. He went first on the first night. When you joined the large crowd pressing its way into the lobby of the theater (it was like a minor-league rock concert), there were cops all over the place. Signs too, forbidding anyone to carry cameras or tape recorders into the theater. Purses, bags, and packages were checked for these possibly dangerous items. It slowed things down a lot, and

Irving started late. He gave a very long reading from a new book. Everybody clapped and went home.

Next night that artist, that old magician Wright Morris, blew the kid away. He came onstage (no nonsense about cameras and tape recorders, only a few benevolent members of the local fuzz in attendance) all dressed in black—black shoes and trousers and a black turtleneck sweater. Under a single spot his wonderful white hair shone and he seemed disembodied, a talking head in midair. His words, all about the writers and the works that had helped him shape his own inimitable voice style, sang in the dark theater, echoed afterward in the wakened minds of all of us.

The rest of us worked in large classrooms in the daytime. At night we went out to Dreamland in the woods for barbecued ribs and beer and Wonder Bread. That's all they served. I remember the late Donald Barthelme looking more than a little puzzled about what he was supposed to do with the ribs and the stack of Wonder Bread. Like a polite missionary at some cannibal feast. He was a Southerner, sure, but a city boy, through and through. I kept waiting and waiting, afterward, for the story that would somehow use Dreamland, the three-hundred-pound black man and his equally large son who owned and managed the place, the ribs and bread, all of it. As far as I know, it never appeared.

Here is what I elected to say at that time in Tuscaloosa, Alabama:

Here are some verses from the middle of the 1940s. Probably about 1946. The teenager, someone who had my name then, not looking much like me at all now, except to my own mother, maybe, being in many ways a complete stranger, save that now, having managed to live longer than he would have dared to imagine possible, or even could have if he had cared to, having changed more, inwardly and outwardly, than his limited imagination or brief flashes of prescience would fortunately permit him to endure in advance—now I can and do understand somewhat, not himself but, anyway, at least some of the reasons he might have written a poem around and about the story of David and Goliath. The mythical meeting of those two was for him an appealing and enigmatic figure, standing for a number of things about life and art, not all of them ineffable. It was, now that I think about it, about style. Among other things.

Here it is again:

Speaking of Minor Revelations
(David and Goliath)
What could be virtue in a giant
is rashness in small boys. The point
beyond which childhood is
calamity is clearly marked.

The giant, standing like a bear,
must be astounded, raise a roar
of natural indignation, or
tilt to laugh at the improbable.

So they must always meet that way,
be disciplined and neat as puppets.
So I must always praise,
with brutal innocence, the accidental.

He's lucky who dies laughing
in the light of it, who leaves
the deft philosophers to argue
that excess is illumination.

David's remarkable disposal of Goliath with sling and found stones has always seemed to me an action that was at once supremely stylish and superbly inappropriate. As for Real Life . . . well, consider that I had (though I had no way of knowing this for certain) just concluded a brief and utterly foolish and absolutely hopeless, though not completely unsuccessful career—I only lost one fight, the last one, after all—as an amateur middleweight fighter, and was about to go off to college, where my next-best main aim and goal was to be a football player. I emerged from the experience of fighting my betters, all of them significantly taller than I, not wiser or much more skilled at it than I had begun, but with a nose that had been broken several times and with teeth that had been shattered one and all to the roots (and yet here I am smiling with them, most of them, still), and I could go away at any time without a mark or scar on my face to show for it. Without applying the lesson specifically to myself, I had learned to be wary of people with unmarked, unscarred faces.

I moved on to play briefly at being a genuine David upon a field full of Goliaths, ruining both knees, breaking both feet, covering my body with cloudy bruises, but more or less holding my own until the arrival of the face mask as a part of the conventional required equipment ruined the one great equalizer that a short, squat pulling guard and middle linebacker could always depend on, namely the fact that nobody, be he ever so big, enormous, gigantic, and huge, likes to get his nose broken and his teeth knocked out. Flying elbows worked no wonders against a face mask. After that, I recollect only long afternoon hours in the steam and stink of a training room and myself hobbling back to the dormitory as swaddled in tape, head to toe, as any decently dressed mummy, reeking of a medley of salves and liniments, groaning (quietly, quietly, smile fixed on face lest anyone suspect my pain) as I passed the tennis courts where crowds of young men all in white and all of them trim and handsome and graceful, not Goliaths, nary a one, but every one an F. Scott Fitzgerald (this was, after all, Princeton); they flaunted what I had to admit was style. I can still hear, at grim will, the keen, crisp sound of tennis balls and rackets meeting each other in autumnal air, can still summon up the slow-fading afternoon light, scent of wood smoke from somewhere, likewise leaf smoke—for they still burned their leaf piles in those days. And in the midst of it all, the boy mummy who would cheerfully have leaped into a burning leaf pile if he could have vanished with the thick, pale gray smoke of it . . . but didn't. Vanished instead, eventually, into the U. S. Army, as a perennial enlisted man, where he learned well how an outward and visible obedient humility can aptly disguise an inward and spiritual exile and cunning. Where he lost the brutal innocence of the aforesaid poem.

As for the poem's style: I can't imagine anymore where it came from, though it certainly seems to suit the fellow who wrote it and who, in his arrogant innocence, would never have imagined himself here and now in such excellent and reputable company, but who also, I must admit in all wistful fairness, wouldn't have cared a whit, one way or the other, if he had been told to expect it. For this to matter at all (and it does matter and I'm grateful to be included here, after all) it was necessary that the arrogant and ignorant innocence be lost, as it was bound to be, and that years of enforced outward and visible humility should slowly teach him a little more cunning, enough to save his skin if not his soul.

A little later, "Speaking of Minor Revelations" was in a book with a company of cousin poems, a book that nobody much liked but Miss Marianne Moore. But that was enough, and she was more than enough for someone who had not (yet), by dint of worldly instruction in humility, joined the man in the ditch waiting for a charitable Samaritan to pass by. The style changed, and yet the next decade, the 1950s, found me—found *him,* I mean—still thinking about David and Goliath, still trying, then, to come to terms with disproportion, still seeking a language and a voice that together could contain both the young shepherd and the giant, the outward and the inward:

Giant Killer

I've heard the case for clarity. I know
much can be said for fountains and for certain bells
that seem to wring the richness from the day
like juice of sweetest fruits, say, plums and tangerines,
grapes and pineapples and peaches. There are so many
ripe things, crushed, will sing on the thrilled tongue.

I know the architecture of the snow's composed
of multitudes of mirrors whose strict forms
prove nothing if they do not teach that God loves all
things classic, balanced, and austere in grace
as, say, Tallchief in *Swan Lake,* a white thing floating
like the feather of a careless angel, dropped.

But there are certain of God's homely creatures that
I can love no less—the shiny toad, a fine hog fat in the
    mud,
sporting like Romans at the baths, a mockingbird
whose true song is like oboes out of tune, a crow
who, cawing above a frozen winter field, has just the
    note
of satire and contempt.

I will agree that purity's a vital matter, fit for
philosophers and poets to doze upon. I'll agree
the blade is nobler than a rock. But then I think
of David and Goliath, how he knelt
and in a cloudy brook he felt for stones.
I like that disproportion. They were well thrown.

And even another one, this one in direct response to a
great artist's vision of the end of the same event, the same
enormous surprise:

David

I think Caravaggio has seen it right,
shown, anyway, with the boy and the head
(Is it really his own face, the giant's,
slack-jawed, tormented? Another story . . .)
the look of the lean boy, the lips
pursed to spit or kiss, the head held high
at arm's length from him by the hair,
the eyes, if they show anything, revealing
pity and contempt, hatred and love,
the look we keep for those we kill.
He will be King. Those fingers twined
in dark will pluck the hair of harps,
golden to make the music of our job
and anguish. By hair will Absalom
dangle from a limb, tongue a thoroughfare for flies,
and this man grown old and soft
will tear his from the roots to make lament.
The look you give Goliath on that day
will flicker in your filmy eyes again
when you spy bare Bathsheba on the roof
(O dark honey, liquor of strange flesh,

to turn a head to birds, a heart to stone!)
and you will live to learn by heart
the lines upon this alien face.
So I am saying Caravaggio
saw it right, that at the moment when
the boy has killed the man and lifts the head
to look at, it is all the beginning and the end.
I, who have pictured this often and always
stopped short of ending, seen David stoop
and feel for smooth stones in the cloudy brook,
the instant when his palm and fist
close like a beggar's on a cold coin,
know now I stopped too soon.
Bathed in light, this boy is bound
to be a king. But the sword . . .
I had forgotten that. A slant
of brightness, its fine edge rests
across his thigh. Never again a rock will do.
It fits his hand like a glove.

By the beginning of the celebrated 1960s that boy and I
had fallen among thieves and we committed more prose than
anything else. I had begun to publish stories and a couple of
novels in the 1950s, prose works that, in the Southern tradition, celebrated the vernacular even as they sought to explore
it. The epigraph for my first book of stories, taken from the
Octavian of Marcus Minucius Felix, says it all: *Non loquimur
magna sed vivimus.* We do not speak greatly. We live. That
was my hope even as it was an assertion. But in the 1960s, I
began to give way to groaning, though I could grit my teeth
in the semblance of a proper grin. I gave way to the vernacular, leaped upon the smoldering leaf pile, and produced a

number of things, including this next little piece on style that comes to us from and through an oddly independent charac- ter named John Towne, about whom a word or two may be helpful if not really necessary. . . . "If the serpent bites before it is charmed, there is no advantage in a charmer" (Eccle- siastes 10:11). Here is something I said about him way back then:

John Towne is essentially a wicked man, worthless as Confederate money, as useless and outdated as a cel- luloid collar. Unfortunately, he is also the protagonist of a novel I have been working on against my better judgment and the judgment of my betters for a very long time. No matter what I try to do, no matter how insulting I am, he will not get lost. However, it ap- pears that I'll have the last laugh on him because (a) it seems highly unlikely that the novel will ever be finished; (b) even if I do accidentally finish it, I am confident that no self-respecting American publisher would ever publish it. Let's hope not. Towne has no redeeming social interest. He couldn't care less. And what makes it really bad is that he is a would-be writer. He is always *expressing* himself. If you'll pardon the expression . . .

Anyway, here is an example of Towne in action with his battered Olivetti and his dreams of glory. It's a mere fragment, of course. That's Towne's genre— the fragment. Fortunately for the health of American letters, he has never been able to finish anything. This subversive lecture was apparently prepared by Towne to deliver to his innocent students at a college where, briefly and under dubious credentials, he held a teaching

job. It is uncertain precisely what college that may
have been. Towne refers to it as Nameless College,
VA, in the hope that he will never get around to de-
livering the lecture there or anywhere else.

Draft for a Lecture on How to Achieve and Maintain a Modern Prestigious Literary Style

Now if you want to sound poetic and literary
and all at the same time, always remember to get
the show on the road with a big, fat, easygoing
dependent clause, holding off the subject for a
good while and letting your participles and your
adjectives do the heavy work for you. Hold back
on the verb for as long as you possibly can. Otherwise it can end up being as embarrassing and
rhetorically disappointing as premature ejacula-
tion. Moreover, this particular method serves to
generate a certain suspense. Which can be a great
help. Particularly if your story doesn't really have
any in the first place. Also it sounds like you
have read a trunkload of foreign books in their
original languages.

I have put together here a very stylish sentence as an example. Of course, it suffers from
being no more (and no less) than a hastily con-
structed pastiche. But nevertheless, I reckon it
will have to do.

Here's how it goes: "Bemused and even perhaps vaguely mysterious behind the smooth *café
au lait* of an unseasonal suntan, the colonel,
clutching his invisible but nonetheless palpable
enigma gracefully about him like a marshal's
splendid cape. . . ."

And next, right here, is where the verb
should come along.

Let's take a look at it. Point of view. We are
observing the colonel from the outside, from a
sort of camera angle. That's good. And there is
an ambiguity about this civilized lens. Which is
also good, in fact very good. Ambiguity is almost
always a good thing in our particular line of
work. In fact, the narrator-observer merely tosses
these perceptions gracefully aside. He's got a million of 'em. Or so it seems.

Notice the use of *"café au lait."* Words in
italics that, upon closer inspection, turn out to be
words or phrases in some foreign language that
the average lazybones may fairly be expected to
know (or anyway recognize) at sight tend to look
good on the page and add status appeal. They
serve to join the reader and the observer-narrator
in a spontaneous yet exclusive club for slightly
world-weary travelers.

"Unseasonal suntan" is a stroke of genius, if
I do say so myself. There it is, just lying there
in the big middle of the sentence like a candy
wrapper or a crumpled Kleenex by the roadside.
Yet it contrives to tell us a whole lot about the
colonel. To begin with, consider this: *He has got
himself a tan at the wrong time of the year.* He
probably uses a sunlamp and probably looks in
the mirror a lot. Or maybe he is always sneaking
off to Florida or the Virgin Islands or Barbados
or somewhere else like that when he ought to be
home and working for a living like everybody
else. In any case, he is a victim of either his own

stupid arrogance or bad taste or both. Metaphori-
cally, which is on the all-important second level,
this teeny little clue lets us know that he may
very well be a bad guy. I mean, he is not natural.
He is a phony. Sun is good and good for you.
Everybody knows that. People who love the sun
and get good natural suntans—excluding, of
course, all those people and races of mankind
who seem to be stuck with permanent suntans of
one shade and the other and who, in most contemporary fiction, are definitely presumed to be
good until it is irrefutably proved otherwise—
people who don't blister or peel or ever have to
rub themselves with Noxzema, sun people are
good people. We all know that. It is an article of
faith.

But mark this well, readers. This cat, this
dude, this jive turkey colonel with his suntan, he
is coming on like he is one of the good people.
Like real, honest-to-God, fun-loving, mankind-
and-nature-loving, right-thinking, liberal, sun-
loving people. And chances are we might not
be able to distinguish him from the real distinguished thing. Except, dear hearts, for that jewel
of an adjective—*unseasonal.* Which our otherwise more or less neutral and objective observer-
narrator has tossed like a gold coin or a piece of
cake into the unruly mob of words. And by that
adjective alone we who know our modern lit
from peanut butter are at least entitled to suspect
that he may be a bad guy who has swiped somebody else's white hat. Oh, he will probably fool

some of the characters in this story, especially the slow-witted ones, but we, ever alert and suspicious readers, shall remain faithfully on our guard.

Now notice some of the other key words— *bemused, mysterious, enigma,* etc. While receiving the observer-narrator's basic signal—"Beats me what's bugging the Bird Colonel!"—we are also getting a side dish of literary class. And we can relax and be safely assured that our observer-narrator has at least gone through *Thirty Days to a More Powerful Vocabulary.* He is definitely a literary type, for (ask anyone) *bemused* is one of your gold-plated, definitely okay *New Yorker*-type literary words.

Note the adverbs. Which are sparingly and judiciously used. Frequent use of adverbs implies a very high degree of intelligence and sophistication. For example, in fiction your average upper-class British character may be expected to throw his adverbs around like they are fixing to go out of style day after tomorrow. This is also true of those Americans who have been to school at Oxford or Cambridge or would like to sound like they might have. As a practical exercise you should stop and count the number of adverbs found in any *New Yorker* story or article, picked at random. You'll see. Chances are you'll find a swarm of killer adverbs anywhere you look.

But let us not sit here smugly and rest content with easy observations. After all, no matter how stylish and decorative it may be, an adverb

is still a functional part of speech. Among a
number of other things, an adverb usually quali-
fies the action of a verb. To qualify something is
to divert attention away from the thing in and of
itself—that is, away from the naked action. An
abundance of adverbs can bring all the action to
a screeching, shuddering halt. Please remember
that all action is, per se, vulgar and commonplace. Or put it another way. You may pick your
nose in public if you must. But always try to do
it with style. Do it with an adverb.

Moreover, since adverbs are, in a sense, the
traveling salesmen of style, they tend always to
make a persuasive case for style even without
seeming to be hustling. Let us suppose, just for
the sake of example, that you were a writer with
absolutely nothing to say—John Updike, for example. Would you confess to your problem and
just quit writing? Hell no, you wouldn't. By the
shrewd and judicious use of all the shell-game
devices of style, you could give content and substance the middle finger and just keep on writing
the same old birdy crapola forever and ever.

Be that as it may, please permit me to call
your attention to another artistic touch, almost
the equal to the brilliant use of *unseasonal.* I am
referring to the clause that reads, "clutching
an invisible but nonetheless palpable enigma
gracefully about him like a marshal's splendid
cape . . ." Now that one is a honey, a real hum-
dinger. That one little word, *clutching,* speaks
volumes. Let's be honest with ourselves. Let's

face it. To clutch anything is to be very crude.
Clutching, like any number of other forms of
grasping, is associated with greed. Also with all
kinds of unseemly urgency and boring desperation. It conjures up a sordid world of ridiculous
social climbers who are not to the manner born.
If you get my meaning. Don't be fooled for even
a minute by all that "invisible but nonetheless
palpable enigma" stuff. This colonel is not only
most likely some kind of a phony, he is also running scared. He is obviously terrified of something. On the other hand, please do not feel that
the other characters in the situation are necessar-
ily low-grade morons or retards just because they
can't see through the colonel. You shouldn't expect them to be as smart and as sensitive as our
narrator-observer, who appears to be willing to
share some of his aperçus with us. Art isn't all
that simple. Many times Art will take you right
out of your shoes. Art will leave you standing
there sucking wind and wondering how you ever
got into this mess in the first place.

Sure he is *clutching* his *enigma*. Why not?
Wouldn't you if you had one? But never mind.
The really important thing is, of course, *how* he
is clutching it. Like a lady with a towel when the
friendly plumber barges into the bathroom without knocking? Like an old man with a shawl
when he feels a chilly draft? Like a miser with a
ten-dollar bill? Like a jack pine high up near
timberline on the sheer edge of a cliff? Like
Harold Lloyd on a window ledge? Like King

Kong holding Fay Wray or Jessica Lange? No, no, a thousand times no! I mean, the man tells us how—"like a marshal's splendid cape." Not Herbert Marshall or E. G. Marshall or R. G. Marshall or General Marshall. Just a marshal, any old marshal. *Gracefully,* too. Graceful is good. Clumsy and awkward are bad. Graceful is what your basic good, natural, liberal, suntanned people usually turn out to be.

Now, then, that cape.

Ask yourself—and I mean this seriously—when is the last time, outside of some old movies, you have actually seen a marshal's cape? For that matter, when is the last time you have actually encountered a marshal? I here exclude federal marshals. There are marshals and marshals. Know what I mean? There is old Marshal Tito, for example, an ambivalent character. There are Hitler's marshals. They were very bad. Except some people like Marshal Rommel, the Desert Fox. Napoleon had marshals, too. Who cares if they were bad or good? Nobody really knows or can remember. Nevertheless, they were French. And they are now long since dead and gone to dust or glory. So, as dead Frenchmen, they can now be glorious, romantic, dashing, brave, doomed, impeccable, splendid, etc.

And thus we are getting the old double whammy. Maybe this colonel is the Hitler type. Or maybe he is Napoleonic. Frankly, I incline toward the former view on the strength of that unseasonal suntan and all the clutching going on.

But only time and a couple hundred pages will tell us for sure. And during that time and those pages we must always allow for the possibility that the aforesaid colonel may change for the better or the worse, or stay pretty much the same, or get dropped out of the story and forgotten about. Anything (or nothing) can happen.

I shall not trouble you by calling attention to such minor and felicitous technicalities as rhythm, assonance and dissonance, alliteration, symmetrical balance, parallelism, and so on, except to point out that they are sure enough all in there, and plenty of them too. Notice that you are approximately halfway through the sentence (go right ahead and count if you want to), all the way up to that word *suntan,* before you even have a clue what the subject of the sentence is.

Is it a bird?

Is it a plane?

Is it Vanessa Redgrave? Linda Evangelista?

Suspense mounts steadily to reach a peak at *suntan.*

"Ah! It's the colonel," we say. "I wonder what the old fart is up to."

Then you have to wait patiently all the way through the second half of the sentence to find out.

Don't hold your breath.

Sooner or later a verb will come winging in and land safely. Just like in German or Latin. Do you remember those good old high-school Latin exercises? "Then having saluted and having bade

farewell to the centurion, from the north gate
riding forth, the south gate being sorely beset
by barbarians, the messenger the letter from the
commander's hand to the emperor bravely sought
to carry."

Or let's try one in Kraut: "Hans Schmerz in
the Black Forest during April near the charming
village of Horsford was born."

Point is, see, if you can screw up an English
sentence sufficiently, you can pass for a college
graduate.

Although it is absent from my own sentence,
the verb nevertheless important and relevant will
prove to be.

Now then, your average writer, who might
be called a run-of-the-mill, blue-collar stylist,
could probably get that far, huffing and puffing.
And then he would probably blow the whole
thing sky-high by introducing an inappropriate
verb. Consider what things the colonel may possibly do and still not violate the context, deco-
rum, dramatical architecture, and syntactical
construction.

What if he:
(a) took off like a big-ass bird?
(b) burped, belched, barfed, and blew lunch?
(c) whistled "Pop Goes the Weasel"?
(d) farted as loud as a slide trombone?
(e) made himself a peanut-butter-and-jelly
     sandwich?
(f) grinned and whinnied like a jackass
     chewing briars?

(g) crossed his eyes and fluttered his tongue
　　 in a loud Bronx cheer?
(h) lit up an exploding cigar?
(i) picked his teeth with a rusty nail?
(j) dropped his trousers and threw a bald
　　 moon at everyone standing behind him?

I shall spare you by ending this list that is already threatening to grow to epic proportions.
From here on, you will just have to take my
word for it. In point of fact, there are only two
things in the whole world that the colonel can
actually do.

He can cough discreetly.

Or he can smile.

I like to think that under the circumstances
he may have smiled. Because smiles are generally
more ambiguous than coughs.

The point is that real style is very hard to
do. And it gets harder and harder all the time.
Everybody keeps jumping in and trying to get
into the act. For instance, all our good, shiny
prestige words keep getting snatched up by politicians and newspaper writers and cheap and
grubby advertising types. Why, those people can
take anything, even a nice, clean, crisp, ordinary
word, one that we all know and love and use all
the time, and in no time at all it will be filthy
and soiled beyond any saving.

Faced with the pitiful and constant corrup-
tion and debasement of his native tongue, the average American writer can only do what he has

always done before and emphatically return to
the strength and energy, the indecorous and
often unbalanced vitality of the living and
breathing and spoken vernacular. And just hope
for the best. . . .

From here on just keep winging until the bell
rings.

—*John Towne*

Came then the 1970s and I, the changing person and writer
calling myself George Garrett, moved on to different places.
To pastures new. I got rid of old Towne by sending him off
first to England then to Africa disguised as an Episcopalian
clergyman, the Reverend R. P. King, that first initial disguis-
ing a first name awarded to him from the Southern vernacular tradition—Radio. Since Towne is a twin, so is Radio,
and his twin brother is named Philco in honor of that wonderful and glowing cathedral shape around and before which
the Towne family, just like mine and maybe even yours, so
often huddled in the evening listening to words of wisdom
and folly from distant worlds.

Anyway, Towne was gone, I thought, for good. Not
knowing how a decade later he would resurface like a killer
whale in a novel called *Poison Pen.* In my innocence of what
the future held in store for me I said then good-bye and good
riddance, except that ne'er-do-well and inwardly shriveled individual did in truth teach me something about how a character, real or imaginary, can create a voice and a style.

Next came forth another kind of character, someone I
had been wrestling with, as Jacob wrestled his angel to earn
a scar and learn his name, ever since the early 1950s—Sir
Walter Raleigh, a giant inwardly and outwardly (he was six

and a half feet tall). When he decides to speak on the subject of style in *Death of the Fox,* it is in the form of an imaginary letter to his real son and heir, Carew, and this letter (later to be burned for the sake of verisimilitude) begins with the abandonment of one kind of style for another:

> My son, it is the prerogative of the old to inflict upon the young the tedious celebration of the past, its spent seasons, festivals, and holidays of lost time. And as the world goes, it falls the duty of the young to hear them out or to seem to, and remains the privilege of the old to practice that prerogative, though the exercise serve only to prove the folly thereof. For the old hold no patent, license, or monopoly on wisdom, which, being mysterious and, all reasonable men agree, invaluable, is beyond the possession of one man or another, one station or one age. For youth, though bound to ignorance out of inexperience, is not likewise condemned to be foolish. For if the purpose of the old be to transmit such wisdom as they deem they have come into, together with a history of themselves and their experience, judiciously framed and arranged in quiet afterthought, and thereby to preserve for the young the best of what has been, and so to defend them from the repetition of many errors and follies of the past, then their intent is surely foolish. It is doomed and fated to fail. The young will either listen, nodding assent and masking an honest indifference, thus learning chiefly the fine art of duplicity at a tender age, or they will listen truly, but without full understanding; as, newly arrived in a foreign country, one listens out of courtesy, and with much frowning concentration,

to a strange tongue, the grammar of which is less than half mastered. Or, should a young man be fortunate enough to be free from need to listen to elders or heed the clucking of old ganders, whose chief claim to excellence is to have lived long enough to be unfit for anything except a stewing pot, he will stop his ears or walk away in insolence, leaving an old man to mutter at his own shadow by the fire.

Nonetheless, with knowledge of the vanity of my purpose and some foreknowledge of its likely failure, I would seek . . .

I would seek . . . what?

A clumsy exercise in antiquated style, lacking the time for revision and polish; so that even if I were not to be credited for any substance whatsoever, I might win grudging approval for virtuosity.

Time will bleed away, an inward wound, until I truly bleed.

If time were blood and an executioner struck off my head now, there would be nothing left in me for a crowd to see. A drained and cured carcass only. For I have been gutted and cleaned and hung up by time like a pig in the cellar. They say—do they not?— that I have the pig's eye. Just so . . . I can find no fault now with that. What is gossip may sometimes be poetry.

"Old men are twice children," the proverb says. Perhaps my son will bear with me for the sake of my second childhood.

You will have noticed that, even as I was bending over my desk writing that down, I was growing as old as Sir Walter Raleigh. Even as I have grown old together with my black-and-tan hound dog, James, named for the last king of the Scots. And now this second time I have just looked up from my desk and the task at hand to find myself and the whole world ten years older and shabbier and worse for wear, my old dog full of yawns and sleep, my children grown up, and myself (except for this present shining moment here and now, where I confess that my literary colleagues, male and female, seem to me as bright and cheerfully glamorous as any Fitzgerald I can possibly imagine)—myself still hobbling past the tennis courts where the lively and the lucky and the imperishably graceful play at their beautiful, bloodless game. And where I was once gnawed with envy I am now stunned with simple admiration.

And so, here and now to conclude things for me is an even older man—one who outlived Raleigh by many years—Sir Robert Carey, first cousin to Queen Elizabeth, a soldier, a gambler, and a seafaring man who, among other things, brought the word to the young King James that the old queen was dead and gone and that he, James, was now to be king of England, France, and Ireland, Defender of the Faith, etc.

Carey, more given to action than contemplation, wrote the only genuine autobiography we have from that whole time. He had just been named Earl of Monmouth in 1626. And here he is, in my novel *The Succession,* as he wakes on the day of that year on which he will begin to write that memoir, composing a passage that ends with the first words of it. This was once upon a time the ending of that novel, though now it exists only here as the end of something else:

Now they are beginning to vanish. As if stepping backward into shadows and stealing away from me.

Slowly and surely. Whose face can that be? The earl says this to himself. Not aloud. Merely mouthing words, tasting them. They seem to describe something he was dreaming only a moment or two before, though what he was dreaming he cannot remember. He was awakened to find himself saying these words without making a sound. Well, why not? There is no one for him to say them to in his bedchamber. No one else here except a young servant boy asleep on a pallet in the dark corner nearest the chamber door. Boy groans something wordless from the deep place of his own dreaming. And then begins to snore.

The moon has long since passed over. And gone down. Could it be any darker in a tomb? He doubts it. And now he thinks he understands why those old pharaohs of Egypt and other heathen and pagan kings and emperors wanted to have their servants buried with them. In a tomb, in the dark of his own grave, the earl would find the groans and snores of the oaf to be deeply reassuring. As they reassure him even now. He smiles to himself, trying to imagine the look on that lout's face if he was told that he was about to be entombed with the earl.

There. Again. Another face. Angry and startled. Whose? What is it?

Soon the last darkness will begin to thin out. Will slowly become gray. Then gray will begin to change until there is the softest hint of rose and pink at the window. Next the cock of the kitchen garden will crow his first doodledoo. Birds in the trees of park and garden will tune and sing. Closer, just beyond the window, he will hear the soft, repetitive, five-note flute sounds of a mourning dove.

Then suddenly all the trumpets of the rising sun.

Well, sun seldom if ever finds him asleep enough to be startled by its arrival. For he sleeps little.

Never has.

When he did doze, eased into sleep a while ago, there were still some patches of gold, faint tatters of moonlight, in the chamber. And the servant, asleep or not, made not a noise. The earl lay still, curtained and softly floating in his four-poster bed. Thinking that he had heard the sound of an owl. Believing that if he lay there, keeping himself very quiet and very still, breathing ever so lightly, he might hear that owl again. Some men fear the owl as the messenger of death and disasters. Well, he has listened for and heard owls for fifty years and still death has not come scratching at his door. Not yet. Meantime, the hoot of an owl can be a great comfort to an old man half awake and with nobody to talk to.

So he lay there content, waiting for the sound. And feeling the smooth, warm, clean texture of the linen sheets, all freshly washed and sunned and aired in this fine weather. Sheets not so fine as were Leicester's, each with his crest and initials embroidered in its corner. But those are gone to rags or to feed moths now, together with the dozens of damask tablecloths he kept in this castle. Well, these are fine enough and clean enough to please a man who once and often slept on cold ground with only wide sky and stars for his covering.

He has not yet permitted himself the luxury of forgetting how that was.

He felt the linen sheets he was lapped in. And breathed the scent of lavender from sheets and pillows.

Which scent he prefers to the saffron that so many folks use. And, feeling himself to be ageless and bodiless, without an ache or pain to his name, he waited for the owl to call again. And so he . . . fell asleep. Into that dream from which he has just now returned. Out of which he was speaking intently to someone. Most likely talking to himself.

There was, though, that face. Remembers that. Indeed can now see it in his mind's eye—a thin, pinched, scarred, crow-trodden, blue-eyed face. Fair-haired, too, but wearing a bloody bandage on his head. But whose? Who is it? Cannot remember.

Well, he could sleep again if he chose to. If he would close his eyes again, breathe in the sweet scent of lavender . . . If it can, as they say, calm and tame a ferocious lion, then why not also an aged and irascible earl.

Could, but he will not. Instead, will stare into the dark and listen for any sounds. And wait for the rising of the sun. Because he has rested enough. Because he can think of nothing else that he is eager to dream of. And, no denying it, because something or other in the dream he was just set free from has left him vaguely troubled and uneasy.

All yesterday was a fine day. Early he was on horseback. In the heat of the morning, before dinnertime, he and the young scholar walked and talked in the garden. Which is much improved already. And now they have been able to repair the pipes and to make that fountain of Leicester's begin its dance again. After a fashion. Heat of the day, but he and his companion stood and talked in the cool mist of the playing fountain. About this and that. About everything.

How it was. How it has been. How it may be. Continued until they were invited in to table. And after dinner with their wine and cheese and fruit and nuts. Until it was time to rest himself a little.

Then, after his napping, he went with some of the others out to the shady green, shadowed from sun by the walls, where they could play at bowling. And where the earl, who has not yet lost his skill at it, made some wagers. And won money from them.

Supper was excellent. Ate lightly, but still had his fill of a good fresh green sallet with herbs, a poached pigeon cooked with berries and fruit, and a fat capon prepared with a sauce of wine and oranges. Finished it with a cold Italian cream and some almond tarts. Washed down by the best and sweetest malmsey he has tasted in some time.

Everything was so well, so delicately cooked that he cannot blame his dream on bad digestion. Which he would not admit to in any case. Lest he should be persuaded of the need for purging. Which he is sure would kill him. These doctors with their purges will kill a man long before his time.

When he dies, let it not be from medicine. Let it rather be from an excess of malmsey, a surfeit of cold Italian cream.

Wonders if Leicester served his guests that dish. And if they found the courage to eat it at his table. No doubt it was worth a poisoning.

Can picture the sudden surprise on a blank face, an imaginary someone or other who has only just surmised that his sweet, cold Italian cream is deadly, is the last sweet thing he will ever eat.

There now. That face again. Face from the dream

returns now. Eyes bulged and popping with surprise and outrage and something more. Eyes clouded with sudden and shadowy knowledge of death. Not death by poison. Not the look of a man who has been sliced or carved with sharp steel. No. This fellow is hanging by the neck. Strangling. Going blue and black in the face.

But it is not the hanging that so astonished and angers him. He was born to hang and knows it. Knew it. Only serious question was when. And where. And by whom.

No. It is more. Pure and angry astonishment of a man who has been badly tricked. And all of a sudden, at one moment (which happens to be his last), knew it.

Very satisfactory for the trickster.

Ah, well.

And now it comes clear whose face was troubling his dream.

Fellow by name of Geordie Bourne. Who else? Scotsman and a thief from birth and a great reiver of the East March.

Taken by some of Carey's men in a bloody little fight. Geordie fought bravely as always. But in a poor place and there were, for once, too many of them for him.

Close friend to Sir Robert Ker, this Geordie was. Who sent word to Carey how he would do a great deal and be willing to give much to save Geordie's hide. And how (also) if means were not found to save his life, why then Ker would bring fire and sword and utter destruction to the English side.

We shall see about that.

His aim at that time was to make mischief for Robert Ker. To teach him something. To shame him. To catch him if he could. So he called a jury. Which promptly found Geordie guilty of March-Treason. And sentenced him to death.

Then waited to see what Ker might do. Whether to hang the fellow or not.

Determined to go and see the fellow with his own eyes. For he and Geordie had not yet met or seen each other face to face.

Here is how the earl will write about it in his memoirs:

"When all things were quiet and the watch set at night, after supper about ten of the clock, I took one of my men's liveries and put it about me. And took two other of my servants with me in their liveries. And we three, as the warden's men, came to where Bourne was kept and were let into his chamber. We sat down by him and told him that we were desirous to see him because we had heard he was stout and valiant and true to his friend. And that we were sorry that our master could not be moved to save his life."

Then they talked a while. And Geordie, a true reiver to the bones, could not help himself from telling them the story of his life.

"Told us that he had lain with at least forty men's wives, some in England, some in Scotland. That he had killed seven Englishmen with his own hands. And that he had spent his whole lifetime in whoring, drinking, stealing, and taking deep revenge for slight offenses."

Geordie asked them if they could send him a minister of the Gospel to comfort his soul. Not that he was in great fear and trembling. But just in case that Ker could not free him and it really came to a hanging.

"I was so resolved that no conditions should save his life. And so I took order that at the opening of the gates on the next morning he should be carried to execution. Which accordingly was performed. . . .

"Came there myself on my own horse to witness the hanging. Which was precisely what caused that memorable look to take command of Geordie's face. Outrage, fury that he had been tricked into confessing (or bragging, if you prefer) his lifetime of sins and crimes. Not to three common and simpleminded Englishmen, as it seemed. But to the very warden, himself. To whom so many (and especially Ker) on both sides of the Border were busily making representation of the excellent character and reputation of the aforesaid selfsame Geordie Bourne and of all the reasons why such a man of good Christian character and decent repute should be spared.

"Oh, it took considerable effort not to laugh out loud at the moment when their eyes met and Geordie Bourne recognized him. And showed that he did with the last living expression of his face.

"Lord, that would have been ill-mannered and unseemly, to laugh in the face of a man you have condemned and who is about to be hanged.

"God's death, the fellow was deeply surprised,

though, was he not? About as much as a man can be. Though only briefly.

"So was Ker surprised. And even more angry. Well, he had time to cultivate his anger. I never knew a man to be so angry about anything as Ker was. You would think he honestly believed that Geordie Bourne would die with his boots off in bed.

"In the end, though, Ker and I became friends. After a fashion. It took some time and some doing, but we finally shook hands on it and even drank to the memory of Geordie Bourne."

Another story. And another story the earl cannot tell his young Oxford scholar. Who, in his youth and high seriousness, will not be able to understand the lighthearted spirit of it. Best not to mention that one. Best to write it down and be done with it. Else Geordie may continue to come into his dreams. And others, too.

Lord, if half the men he has had to hang (for their own good and the good of the Border) return to people his dreams, his nights will be more crowded with faces than the Court at Christmastime. And such ugly faces. Wonderful, rough, and everlastingly ugly faces.

He thinks it might be rude and unseemly even now to laugh out loud in the privacy of his own bedchamber. Yet he cannot suppress it anymore.

And his laughter fills the room. Startles the servant awake.

And so begins another summer's day.

Well, the trick has turned on him now. He can delay and procrastinate no longer.

Time has come to tune or play the lute. To write it down and forget about it.

Pens sharpened. Inkhorn and paper and plenty of fine sand for plenty of blotting.

No more excuses or diversions.

Robert Carey, Baron of Leppington and Earl of Monmouth, must and will begin to write his memories.

He will begin, as is the oldest custom, with a prayer: "Oh Lord, my God, open mine eyes and enlarge my heart with a true understanding of Thy great mercies, that Thou has blessed me withal, from my first being until this my old age. And give me of Thy grace to call in mind some measure of Thy great and manifold blessings that Thou hast blessed me withal. Though my weakness be such and my memory so short, as I have not abilities to express them as I ought to do, yet, Lord, be pleased to accept of this sacrifice of praise and thanksgiving. . . ."

Tigers in Red Weather

Some Academic Anecdotes

People are not going
To dream of baboons and periwinkles.
Only, here and there, an old sailor,
Drunk and asleep in his boots,
Catches tigers
In red weather.

                    —Wallace Stevens,
        "Disillusionment of Ten O'Clock"

If you were to take a look at my résumé, you would see at once that it is built mostly around my life and career as a teacher. It leaves out a lot of things. One of these is the whole list of jobs, mostly menial and manual, that I, like so many others in and of my generation, have worked at in youth and during hard times when I couldn't find a teaching job. I don't want to spend much time describing those things. Except to repeat that they were more or less usual for only slightly skilled people of my age and generation. I have worked at loading and shipping. I have been the driver and operator of various kinds of vehicles. I have, in my time, installed a lot of linoleum and ceramic tile. I have worked in construction for contractors—mostly at toting and fetching, hewing and drawing. Once upon a time I earned some pretty good money as a bartender, working with a crew who performed our tasks and chores at large parties for the very rich.

None of this was for very long. It is a matter of no special importance except that you learn how to work (at anything) by working at everything that comes along.

If you happen to come along, in my family, during a depression, you learn to make your own way, as best you can. You do not live a sheltered life. You are not in the least ashamed of working with your hands and muscles at tasks that don't require a lot of skill. You admire and honor others, the workers with real skills, earned and learned. But you are not sentimental about work and working people.

One day when the chance comes along (the GI Bill and a fellowship nobody else wanted at the time) to go to graduate school and, you hope, into teaching, you take that chance. And even at its worst (and some of the worst people I have ever met are holed up and hunkered down in the academies—alas, teaching our children, who deserve better), you never forget what it is like to put in a long hard day's work with back and biceps and then to try to write poems and stories and anything else in your spare time. You have some pride. You have done it and, Lord willing, you could do it again, you think. But meantime, all things considered, the life of a teacher-writer has advantages and privileges.

It isn't quite as good as the way it was described by an old lady, a kinswoman of your wife.

"Oh, how I envy you!" she said when I told her I was going to graduate school, aiming to be a teacher. "Academic people go through life so gently."

Take that, as I did, as a joke. A middle-of-the-night teeth-gnasher. Nevertheless, in a relative sense (and what other sense is there?) it's the truth.

As for the books. Well, for better and for worse, they are who I am.

One day, thirty years ago or thereabouts, Shelby Foote came to my creative writing class at the University of Virginia. He talked a little while, then answered questions. Knowing that Foote had known William Faulkner, one of the students asked Foote what Faulkner was really like.

"Have you read the books?" Foote asked.

"Yes, sir."

"Well, that's who he is. That's all there is."

Wesleyan University
(1957–1960)

Gadfly

At the Faculty Meeting I saw him bleed
for Nonconformity and, good classicist, bare
all his wounds, calling on us to rise, rebel,
to shrug the yoke, come down from bitter cross.

The President, I noticed, was impassive,
attentive and indifferent as a *croupier.*
Not the least fault or fissure of emotion
troubled the contours of his familiar smile.

Now this is Ancient History.
We live and learn.

The Gadfly was promoted while
Rebels were scattered like a covey of quail
in everywhich direction.
Folding their caps and gowns like Arab tents,
they muttered, "Tar and feathers," fled.

Now over coffee, steaming rich
subsistence of the academic nerve,
I hear him say: "What we need
is less of milk and honey and more of sting.
Things hereabouts are whitewashed. Let us
act. A little water clears us of the deed.
And what do you think?"

I smile and shrug.
I pay the check and plead a class
and leave him talking still,

safe in the shadow of his Great Man,
a trim Diogenes in tub of honest tweed.

Show Biz
(1960)

I was still teaching at Wesleyan then, a beginning teacher too. Agent called from New York and said to be there in the city at a time and place. There was a chance we could sell a story to TV and perhaps even get the right to adapt it. Brand-new series looking for new young writers. Arrived. He seemed relaxed, matter-of-fact, loose, and cool, for a man with a tough selling job. Up a shiny, pilotless elevator to the dim heights of a building. Down corridors, past Guards and shiny Receptionists. Through a room, awkward and noisy, that seemed full of all kinds of freaks. Impression of a trio of midgets juggling, a child in Fauntleroy outfit practicing a tap dance, a very fat woman, sheet music in her lap, her hands soft and folded demurely in her lap. Beautifully patient. Impression of several nervous little round men. Equally nervous lean and gray ones. A large Negro smiling to himself and fooling with a harmonica. A fading blonde touching up her makeup at a mirror. A room packed, smoky, noisy, rich, and redolent with the odor of humanity. It could have been a sealed boxcar rolling east. A glance only at the inevitable Receptionist as we simply passed through the room. She neither cool nor shiny. Not likely to smile even if we did have the right murmured name or card. In fact ignoring us, as we entered from one blank door, crossed the room briskly with the Agent in the lead, and went out through another blank door. She ignoring us, though no one else did. Questions, judgment, indignation, injustice, worry in their eyes. We might be anybody. Or nobody . . . A glance at her as she ignored our passing. Neither cool nor shiny. Granite instead, roughly, carelessly chipped and hewn. Glass-eyed, utterly indifferent. Silent with the repose of a jagged rock. You would never speak to her unless spoken to.

We closed the door behind us. Another little hall. The Agent stopped, leaned close and confidential. Which was his way, always, even if only to ask the time of day or to remark on the weather.

"The show is new and hasn't got permanent space yet," he said. "We have to go through the waiting room for that talent-scout show."

This an afterthought, after the experience.

"Is that where they get the talent?"

"No," he said. "It's all set up, but they have to go through the motions, you know."

"You mean none of those people will ever get on the show?"

A look not so much of scorn as of genuine astonishment. Perhaps I was slow-witted.

"Did you see those creeps?" he asked. Then to my nod: "They go through the motions. It's like—public relations."

"Do they know that?"

"If they don't, it's their own fault."

The American Academy
(Rome, 1958–1959)

At teatime in the living room every afternoon a very old gentleman emerged from the depths of the library and, not speaking to anybody else, indeed not really seeming to notice anyone else, had a cup of tea, cream, and two lumps of sugar, and nibbled on a macaroon. When he finished his tea and cookie, he would produce a large gold watch, lean close to look at it. Then totter away out of the Academy toward the street.

He fascinated me. I had never, still haven't, seen anyone that old and frail up and moving around. The suit he wore was of a cut and style I had never seen before except in places like pictures of the people at the Columbian Exposition of 1893 in Chicago. His wing collar and necktie looked like President Woodrow Wilson's.

He was the Mystery Professor to me. Came every week-day in the morning. Descended into the depths of the library, emerging in time for tea in the afternoon.

Nobody was quite sure what he was working on, but whatever it was, it had kept him busy from about 1920 to the present. Every day he came up the Gianicolo from Rome on a crowded bus, spent the day at work, had tea, then went back home, wherever that was, on another crowded bus.

"He has had his pockets picked many times," someone told me, someone who seemed to know. "They get his money, but they haven't gotten that gold watch yet."

"What happened during World War II?" I asked.

Turns out that's the best part, this someone, who seemed to know, told me. At the outbreak of war between the U.S. and Italy, the Americans all went home and the Swiss were in charge here. They just had a maintenance staff. Nobody *used* the building. Except. You guessed it. The Mystery Professor. He came on the bus every weekday. Descended into the depths of the library. Emerged at teatime and . . .

"Don't tell me the Swiss served him tea."

"Not at first. He would come up to the living room and look all around and wait and wait before he looked at his watch and left. He seemed genuinely befuddled that there was no tea tray, no servant in a white coat to serve him a cup of tea. He never said anything, of course. But he looked confused and upset."

So the Swiss served him tea every afternoon for the rest of World War II. And he went on doing his work. Whatever it is.

"I wonder if he noticed that there was a war on."

"I very much doubt it. Why would he? Oh, he must have wondered once in a while as governments and armies came and went. But he had his work to do (whatever it may be). And the rest of the world, in peace or at war, was without much meaning. Of course, the world picked his pockets from time to time. But otherwise the world left him alone."

The Alley Theater
(Houston, Texas, 1960 – 1962)

My time as a kind of playwright-in-residence (together with Richard Wilbur) at the Alley was wonderful for me.

Meeting and getting to know a whole troupe of talented actors; following a dozen or so plays from first reading to final performance; above all having a year to work with the late Nina Vance, one of the truly great and gifted American directors of our time.

I did a couple of plays for them. *Garden Spot, U.S.A.* for adults and *Sir Slob and the Princess* for children. *Garden Spot* had a nice run there and then died quietly and mercifully. *Sir Slob* is still being performed, thirty years later, in children's theaters all over the country.

Truth is, it was the children's theater at the Alley that interested me most. I took a couple of my children there every Saturday morning to see a play. It was exciting (and instructive) to experience theater in a crowd of a few hundred restless and demanding children.

One time, I remember, I took my son Bill to see a version of *Hansel and Gretel.* It was well done, more than a little scary, and kept him deeply involved.

At one point the witch put Hansel and Gretel into a cage and hooked them in.

When she left them and left the stage (it was theater in the round) Bill jumped up and ran out onstage. Unhooked the cage and held the door for them.

"Run!" he cried. "Run!"

Just then the witch returned and scared him back into his seat.

There was lots of participatory interaction (as they say). That's what I liked best about children's theater.

On the opening night of *Garden Spot,* my other small son, George (up past his bedtime, to be sure), blurted out, audibly: "Daddy, it's just like your children's play!"

That was intended as a compliment. The local critics heard it and took note of it in their reviews.

Rice University
(1961 – 1962)

I was already in Houston, working at the Alley Theater and, as it happened, living only a few blocks from Rice in the little enclave of West University, when Rice needed somebody to teach a couple of English courses on very short notice. I think somebody or other had quit just before the fall term got under way. But I don't really know what happened to create a job for me. I never asked.

Rice seemed like a wonderful little school. Small-college atmosphere in the big middle of a city. I would walk over from my house three days a week, pick up any mail at the English office, teach my classes, and meet with students for tutorials and conferences in the student center. The kids were overworked and tired most of the time. The whole thing was free in those days, but a student could be expelled (there was a waiting list for every place and slot) for falling behind or low grades. They came and went. Sometimes I would cut through the campus coming back from a play or a concert or the movies or a party in downtown Houston. And at two o'clock in the morning all the lights in all the dorms would be burning. They studied all the time.

But the students were good (not *adventurous,* but good) and my colleagues left me happily alone. And the schedule was easy, really no more than an interruption in my writing day.

Best of all Rice seemed to have next to no bureaucracy, almost no paperwork. Every other school I knew of was a blizzard of papers—memos to read and answer, forms to fill out, reports to make or to comment on. There was hardly ever anything in my departmental mailbox.

I told my colleagues, whenever we did get together over coffee or something, how lucky they were to work at a wonderful school that had eliminated most of the paperwork that was smothering American education.

They smiled and shrugged and looked a little odd. Of course, they didn't really have anything to compare it with. They probably couldn't appreciate how remarkably free they were.

Things were so loose and causal that at the end of the first semester I didn't receive any grade sheets from the registrar's office. I went there and checked in, explaining my problem. They assured me that they had sent out some grade sheets for my classes, but maybe they had been lost or something. They were very polite and considerate (amazingly so for academic administrators, who tend to cultivate rudeness to faculty as a perk of their jobs, part of their job descriptions) and I left convinced that Rice was unique in the simplicity and decency of its administration. A model for every other college and university in America. I said this to my colleagues also. And, as before, they smiled oddly and shrugged.

Came the end of the year. Last class. I taught it, then dropped by the English department to see if there was anything—final grade sheets maybe—in my mailbox. Nothing much. I turned and encountered the chairman, whom I had actually seen in person about twice during the whole academic year.

We exchanged idle pleasantries, indulged in small talk.

Then he said: "I do hope you and your wife are going to come to our party on Thursday night."

"Well, sir," I told him, "we would certainly like to and we will if we can. This is the first I've heard about it."

"That can't be," he said. "I sent you at least three notices about the party."

"Well, I'm sorry. I never got any of them."

"That's strange."

I was getting mildly annoyed at the whole thing.

"I come here regularly Monday, Wednesday, and Friday to teach my classes. I always come here to the department and check the mailbox. And I never got anything about any kind of a departmental party."

"Oh," he said. "I wouldn't have sent it here. I sent it to your office."

"My office? I don't have an office."

"Sure you do," he said. "Everybody has an office."

"I don't."

After a little more of this he got a key and led me over to the library, then down to the basement.

Pretty soon we were standing in front of a door with my name stenciled on it. He opened the door and we pushed our way inside. Pushed, had to, because the whole room was a huge pyramid of paper. Official letters, memos, forms to be filled out, reports to be made. Piles and piles. Copies of copies. Some stamped Final Notice. Others bearing savage warnings of what I might expect if I did not reply at once and forthwith.

I stood and laughed a while. He gave me the smile and the shrug. Closed and locked the door. We walked outside together.

By the time we were in sunlight and shade I had time to think a couple of things about all this.

First thing I realized was that I had failed not just occasionally, but completely. In terms of the bureaucracy and paperwork I had done nothing, *zero*, right all year long. So? Nothing had happened to me or my students or the school. All was well.

Next thought I had was to picture it from *their* point of

view. There's this guy, this one fella over there in the English department, who is absolutely and completely uncooperative. He won't do anything right. Or wrong, either. Won't do anything except teach his classes. What's wrong with him? What the fuck is he trying to prove? Must be crazy. Send him a memo. Send him another warning.

The University of Virginia
(1962 – 1967, 1984 –   )

To make sense out of the experience of UVa you have to understand how the university itself is constantly growing and changing its spots and its nature, yet always around the virtually unchanged center of the grounds, the Rotunda, the lawn, the gardens, the ranges (east and west), all designed by and built for Thomas Jefferson and still kept pretty much the way he wanted them to be. Which is to say that there have been many outward and visible changes. Even since my first time there—1962 to 1967. Back then, before the uproar of protesting students really caught on nationwide and became (briefly enough, thank God; it all ended as if somebody had flipped a switch when they stopped the draft) an academic fashion like Spring Break at Fort Lauderdale, UVa still had a coat-and-tie dress code. Rebels wore no socks. And it was still not coeducational. Now there are more women than men and, as far as I can tell, no dress code of any kind except that somehow everyone seems to have on the same things at the same time. In that sense it is no different than, say, VMI, which has a uniform of the day. Somehow without benefit of bugle calls or garbled announcements on PA systems the UVa students, especially the young women, all manage to put on the same things at the same time. Since a lot of them look very much alike, anyway, falling into several basic models (one, for example, your basic Bow Head, is an interchangeable chunky blonde with a ponytail), I find myself wondering how they tell each other apart. Indeed, sometimes they seem so very much alike I wonder how they can be sure of their own names and identities.

There are five times as many students now as there were in the 1960s, and (truth is) they are a more diverse crowd, reflecting the diversity of the larger society. But at heart, often unbeknownst to the new actors on the old stage, inwardly and spiritually it remains the same place it always was.

The Shelby Foote story tends to make precisely that point.

When I first arrived at UVa the famous scholar Fredson Bowers was running the English department. With a heavy hand, if not an iron one. He was an effective administrator, but finesse was not his strong suit. Neither was tact. Most of the untenured teachers were scared to death of him. He used to threaten to send miscreants off to our extension in Clinch Valley, remote in those days, in southwest Virginia. And he actually did assign a few young instructors there.

One of his first assignments to me was to get us a week-long writer-in-residence. Someone who could come and give a couple of public lectures and meet a bunch of classes. Someone who would draw a nice crowd at the MacGregor Room of the library to justify the expense and the idea of a visiting writer. Over the past few years, he told me, the audiences for this kind of thing had dwindled to a hard-core few who came as much for the booze at the reception afterward as anything else.

My assignment was to use the lordly inducement of four hundred dollars, plus room and board, to bring a well-known writer to UVa, as soon as possible, for a week. I gulped and told him I didn't know of any writer who would come here for a week for a fee like that. Nonsense, he told me, saying that William Faulkner only got three hundred dollars for a whole semester.

He handed me a list of writers to try. Mostly *New Yorker* people. Bowers was married to the story writer and novelist Nancy Hale, who was often published in the *New Yorker* in those days.

Top of the list was John O'Hara. As a pedagogical device, to teach Bowers the way of the world, I wrote a cheerful letter to Mr. O'Hara offering him this wonderful opportunity to come to UVa, stressing the Faulkner connection and the fact that O'Hara's honorarium would be more than Faulkner's. I then showed the letter to Bowers before I mailed it. It looked fine to him.

Back it came, with like a one-day turnaround, my own letter with a huge "FUCK YOU!" scrawled across it.

Bowers professed to be baffled by that reaction.

"John is probably hard at work on a new novel or something," he said. "Try the others."

In no time everybody else on his list had replied with firm if more polite refusals.

"See if you can find somebody," Bowers commanded.

"Yes, sir."

I looked around. Didn't know Shelby Foote personally at that time. But I did know that the second volume of his huge masterwork, *The Civil War,* had just been published. And I also knew that he was scheduled to be in Washington, D.C., attached to the Arena Stage under a Ford Foundation Grant. I made contact with him and discovered that, remarkably, he was available because his wife and family were still in Memphis and the apartment he had found in Washington would not be ready for a couple of weeks. A week at UVa would be fine and dandy under the circumstances. Sure, the four hundred dollars was pretty slim pickings, but, together with meals and a place to stay, it beat living in a hotel in Washington.

Excited at my big catch, I went straight to Bowers. Who was not happy or amused.

"You have made a mistake and you have wasted four hundred dollars of the department's money," he said. "But maybe you can learn something from the experience.

"You see," he continued, "it's a matter of visibility, publicity, here on the grounds and all over the state. I am sure this person—Foote, did you say his name is?—is a fine writer and all that. But nobody ever heard of him. Nobody will come to the MacGregor Room to hear him. It's a complete waste of money."

Long pause as if the great man were deep in thought. "We're committed to this person?"

"Yes, sir."

"Well, then. Make the best of it."

I left, gnashing my teeth. Foote was one of the few living American writers whose work I admired without any hint of doubt or reservation. Grimly I determined to prove Fredson Bowers wrong.

First, publicity. I had a batch of glossy photographs of Foote (that wonderful bearded face that looks like it lived through the Civil War) run off. I put together a release with the basic information about him and the gig at UVa and wrote an accompanying letter, explaining that I was just a poor and humble instructor of English, unfamiliar with the ways and means of public relations and under pressure from my boss to earn some space and attention for this forthcoming event. I then stressed the importance of Shelby Foote in contemporary American literature, pointing out that this was a rare visit to an academic institution on his part and his first visit to the University of Virginia.

Within a couple of days his face and a fine story were on the front page of every newspaper in Virginia. Over in Richmond the *Times-Dispatch* ran an editorial complimenting the university on its choice for a writer-in-residence. Through some old buddies who were reporters I managed to get some coverage ("Foote Goes to UVa") far afield, including the *Houston Post, Houston Chronicle,* even, Lord save us, the *San Francisco Chronicle.* I bought a scrapbook, cut out clippings, and sent it off to Bowers. He sent for me.

"Publicity is one thing," he said. "But true visibility is another. Wait and see what kind of a crowd you get."

He went on to tell me that I was in big trouble because I had dealt directly with the newspapers instead of going through channels, through Information Services.

"Sorry about that," I said. "I didn't know we had an information office."

"Never mind," he said. "I told them you are new and don't know any better."

Lordy, Lordy, Lordy . . .

The crowd thing really did have me worried, though. It would be embarrassing and a big shame if Bowers proved right and I couldn't turn out a good crowd for Foote. I was sure that once he was here, seen around and about on the grounds, went to some classes and so forth, the word would get out and he would be a popular lecturer. But Bowers was right about one thing—I was brand-new here, didn't know how things worked.

I decided to hedge my bet with a little P. T. Barnum action.

I had a bunch of football players in my second-year survey of English literature course, a required course. "How would you guys like to get a guaranteed B in this course?" I asked them. That seemed like a pretty good idea to them. I asked them to act as ushers for the lecture and maybe to see if they could round up a few people to usher around. Fine by them.

There was a graduate student who played trumpet, very well, and had a Dixieland band. I hired him and his band to come and play a little warm-up concert in front of the library, starting about half an hour before Foote's lecture, hoping that it might help swell the crowd. So that Shelby Foote would miss all of this, I arranged for some attractive students to take him to supper downtown (or out of town) and to arrive back just in time for the lecture.

The day of the lecture, scheduled for 8:00 P.M., I paid for an ad in the student newspaper, the *Cavalier Daily*. It was the age of "happenings." I decided we needed one. My ad was simple. It said:

SOMETHING WILL HAPPEN

RIGHT SMACK IN FRONT

OF ALDERMAN LIBRARY

TONIGHT AT 7:15 P.M.

BE THERE.

Sure enough, starting at about 7:15 that evening a good-size crowd gathered in front of the library. The band arrived and unpacked their instruments. They had just started playing when it began to rain. They stopped and packed up again.

"Wait!" I cried. "Maybe it will stop raining or something."

Fat chance. It was pouring.

Just then a young woman, a wonderfully good-looking

young woman who was on duty at the circulation desk of the library, came running out and invited everybody to come on inside and get out of the rain.

"Nobody's here," she said. "It's as quiet and boring as a tomb. Come on in and play me some music."

And they did that.

And after a few numbers everyone, band and large crowd, got carried away. Fell into single file, a regular P-rade, and marched all through the stacks of the library, playing Dixieland jazz, clapping, and cheering.

Ended up in the basement, in the MacGregor Room. Where my huge football players, all in dark suits and wearing dark glasses, shut the doors behind them and then planted themselves against the doors to keep the crowd in place. And what a crowd it was in the MacGregor Room! It was already full, packed, in fact, before we came in with the band and its bunch. Now it was certainly unsafe, probably unhealthy. Outside, at the street entrance, there was another huge crowd, pushing and shoving, trying to get in. Later I heard that Bowers and a couple of other senior professors couldn't get within fifty yards of the place.

Foote arrived and received an enthusiastic standing ovation. Almost everybody was already standing up anyway. So why not? They were very responsive. Laughed with unusual enthusiasm at even the least of his jokes.

It was a triumph.

Next day I dropped by Bowers's office, hoping to rub it in a little. Very humbly and politely, of course. Of course. But before I had a chance to say anything at all (like: "We missed you at the lecture, sir"), he tossed me the *Cavalier Daily,* which had a story about the complaints of several distinguished scholars, led by an ancient and emeritus professor

of some obscure discipline, that their quiet and peaceful studies were interrupted by a blaring band and a mob of scream-
ing undergraduates who, without rhyme or reason or
discernible purpose and evidently led by a young instructor
in the English department, took over the library for half an
hour. Barbarians! Visigoths! "Never since Mr. Jefferson's day
has any such thing happened at this great institution! . . .
Blah, blah, blah!"

"I thought you wanted visibility, sir," I said lamely.

He didn't even bother to answer.

But the subject of this little anecdote (surely you still remember?) was how at UVa everything seems to change and
nothing ever really changes.

Cut to 1987.

I have now had twenty years of a life elsewhere. Am now
back at UVa as the Henry Hoyns professor of creative writing. A chair and a title. Well, a guy who would follow a jazz
band through a library would fall for a title and a chair at
the scene of the crime, wouldn't he? Anyway, I am back.
Bowers is long since retired. The chair, at this moment in '87,
is an Englishman.

Anyway, new chairman, new English department, except
for a handful of old-timers, and I'm back in the job.

I am informed by the chair that a prominent alumnus
with literary interests, one Michael Rea, has given the department five thousand dollars, on a one-year trial basis, to invite
a writer-in-residence to come for a week. Attend some classes
and give a public lecture or reading. Do I have any suggestions?

Matter of fact, I do. Shelby Foote.

Oh . . . Well, could I furnish the chair some material
concerning this person? Did I say Foote?

Certainly. And I put together a package and take it to him.

Time really has passed. In this day and age five thousand dollars, for a "name" writer, is about like Bowers's four hundred. People I know of, like Ann Beattie, Toni Morrison, Tom Wolfe, etc., are running around getting more than twice that much just for a one-night stand, a reading. I am guessing, betting that *maybe* I can get Shelby Foote out of friendship and sentiment. Of course, it looks easy at this énd. Prominent people in other departments have written me in strong support of the idea.

After a while I get back a letter from the chair politely declining my advice and counsel. He fears that the donor will not want to continue the program "if he thinks we are not trying to bring in the best and brightest" and adds a bit of pragmatic wisdom: "Politically, I think it would be wise to get the program established by bringing in big names for the first couple of years, before turning to those equally (or even more) deserving who are, for whatever reason, less well and widely known."

Everything changes. Everything stays the same.

Less well and widely known, huh?

I hope you happened to see "The Civil War" on PBS.

Dixieland bands and ancient professors whose quiet studies are interrupted lead me directly and briefly to the next two anecdotes.

Hollins College
(1967–1971)

As far as I know, to the best of my recollection, Hollins was almost untouched by the campus riots and uprisings near the end of the Vietnam War. A philosophy class sat down and blocked access to the only handy government installation—the campus post office. There was a quiet candlelight march around the quadrangle one evening. There were a couple of angry and mostly incoherent letters to the student paper. And that was about it. Except for one time, one event.

One time the whole student body got well worked up by something they read in the paper or saw on TV. They milled around the quadrangle for a while, then decided to march on the president's house and make some demands.

The president, John Logan, was a very nice, charming, and convivial fellow. One thing he did for fun and games was play (clarinet, I think) in a Dixieland band composed of faculty and staff, a band (it once featured the famous Louis D. Rubin, Jr., on harmonica) called the Hambones. On the evening in question, when the students marched, forming a noisy mob in front of his house, he happened to be playing with the rest of the band in his living room. Went outside to greet them. Told them he would be glad to listen to any and all demands and to discuss things with them.

"But first," he said, "let's have a little music."

The band came out on the front porch and began to play. They played and played. Some say they never played so well before or since. Anyway, it wasn't very long before they had the young women of Hollins College first swaying with the beat, then dancing around, finally dancing away in all different directions.

They forgot about why they had come there in the first place.

When the last of them had gone off into the dark, the president and his buddies went back inside, had a few drinks, and started in playing away at the old familiar tunes again.

Out on the Circuit

Randall Jarrell was apparently convinced there was a star poet out on the lecture circuit, a kind of poetic Kilroy whose name was Manny Gumbo. Wherever you yourself went to lecture and read your poems, Manny had always been there just before you.

Everybody is always eager to tell you all about it. You step from your bus or airplane, blinking and travel-weary, and they greet you with the news of it.

"Manny Gumbo was just here. What a show! He arrived wearing a top hat. That's *all* he was wearing. And when he left here, two sororities chartered buses to follow after him. Forever and ever, I guess. You know how *he* left here? He drove off in a tank he stole from the ROTC armory and with a brand-new punk-rock band he put together while he was here—the Running Anapests!"

The nickel-and-dime poet travels light, unburdened by the baggage of reputation and legend. With only the words of the poems to stand by and for and on. Travels light and alert, ready for a checklist of things that will more than likely happen.

Each institution, be it ever so humble, will have at least one local poet whose open indifference and public yawns of overwhelming ennui must be expected and understood.

Always from some of the brighter students and bitter junior faculty will come devastating smirks, followed by difficult and tricky questions.

There are always drinks, and every swallow will be closely watched and duly noted.

There will be a dinner, usually at "the only half-decent place in this town—you'll be amused by its pretentious ambience." To be eaten in raw haste: "Don't feel pushed or anything, but we have to be back at school in twenty minutes."

There is soon the stomach-churning rush from dinner to

the lecture hall. "Don't worry, ha-ha, they can't start without us."

Afterward there will be the Party. With the ordeal of public performance behind you, you are feeling a little light-headed and manic. Ready to party. But you are soon reminded that for all these other people, your hosts, it is their umpteenth identical affair this semester. That they are all very tired, tired of you, tired to death of each other, tired already in tedious anticipation of the classes they must teach or attend tomorrow. Someone slips you an envelope (if you are lucky) with the check in it. And then, all of a sudden, everyone is leaving or long gone.

Maybe there was a little bell ringing and you missed it.

Sometimes, unwisely, you wind up in the local poet's kitchen, voices muted lest we wake the sleeping children, swapping drunken, thick-tongued memories and miseries and war stories until the dawn's early light begins to break.

Or, back at the witching hour, somebody is dragooned into driving you and dropping you off at the haunted motel. It is never the most beautiful young woman at the Party who does this service. She spent twenty minutes breathlessly telling you how much she loves the poetry of Manny Gumbo.

Dawn, and you are off again. Muttering stomach and muttered grunts of farewell from the low-ranking lad whose lot it is to see you safely to the airport or the bus station. You are now feeling cotton-tongued, laced together with shrinking rawhide and buttons of pain, stem to stern.

You have carried the flag of your employing institution. You have done your best. You feel like a fool.

None of it is worth the lonely, silent privilege of writing one good line of poetry.

Even Manny Gumbo knows that much.

Princeton 1
(1964 – 1965, 1973 – 1975)

Or Death and December
The Roman Catholic bells of Princeton, New Jersey,
wake me from rousing dreams into a resounding
     hangover.
Sweet Jesus, my life is hateful to me.
Seven A.M. and time to walk my dog on a leash.

Ice on the sidewalk and in the gutters,
and the wind comes down the one-way street
like a deuce-and-a-half, a six-by, a semi,
huge with a cold load of growls.

There's not one leaf left to bear witness,
with twitch and scuttle, rattle and rasp,
against the blatant roaring of the wrong-way wind.
Only my nose running and my face frozen

into a kind of a grin that has nothing to do
with the ice and the wind or death and December,
but joy pure and simple when my black-and-tan puppy,
for the first time ever, lifts his hind leg to pee.

Princeton 2

Professor of Belles Lettres
His book-lined study ought to be a TV set.
Some very nice first editions in alphabetical order and
     himself fully armed by J. Press,
chain-smoking while he conducts a class—
"The Growth of National Consciousness in American
     Lit."

There's a picture window with a view
of barbered green lawn and a man with a lawn mower.
"Italians love to cut grass," his wife said.

Afterward there is tea,
during which he collects
the latest undergraduate slang
in an indexed notebook.

I do not know if he believes in anything
or has any love by which he lives
but, over the shine of the teacups
and the glint of the silver service,

have seen tears in his eyes
when he talked about Sacco and Vanzetti or the peace
of Walden Pond.

University of South Carolina
(1971 – 1973)

I reckon I know dozens, maybe hundreds, of literary anecdotes about James Dickey. That's because I collect them. So
do many others, all of us fans of his poetry and his inimitable
self-image-making, and sometimes we all get together and
spend a happy hour or two just swapping Dickey stories, the
new ones and some of the old ones. Someday we are going
to have a conference somewhere and just tell Dickey stories.
Part of it will be Dickey imitations. Among the writers of
whom any one is a potential finalist in a James Dickey im-
personation contest are: Richard and Robert Bausch, Henry
Taylor, Franklin Ashley, James Seay, Joseph Maiolo, and, of
course, Ben Greer. Maybe we can persuade Dickey himself to
judge and pick the winner. Greer, a fine novelist who teaches

at South Carolina and was, once upon a time, my student and Dickey's too, is the source for the final scene of this one. . . .

Greer was visiting me in Maine. One day, sitting on the front porch, watching the tide in the York River flow in and ebb out (which is the principal activity of any given day), we were tossing back a few and reading magazines and stuff. And one or the other of us found a story in the latest *Time* magazine. Which began, as I recollect, like this: " 'He cursed and reviled me and stated that it was his intention to whip my ass,' testified South Carolina Highway Patrolman L. J. Tippet. . . .'" Etc.

Story was that poet James Dickey, wakened from a snoring sleep amid the wreckage of his totaled Land Rover, which he had run into a large tree, came out swinging and cussing. There wasn't a whole lot to the story except that a very prominent poet had gotten somewhat inebriated, and sometime between four A.M. and a little after five A.M., when the cops happened by, he had plowed into a tree on a quiet residential street. Nobody noticed. Dickey wasn't hurt (for once he'd remembered to buckle up his safety belt). He just hung there, all snarled up in the belt, and fell asleep until the cops came along.

Pretty soon both Ben and I had a lot more material to consider. Friends who knew we cared sent us clippings from the South Carolina papers and even the *Washington Post* (which stated that, according to blood and breathalyzer tests, Dickey was the drunkest human being ever picked up in the state of South Carolina; who knows?). From friends and all the coverage, we learned that Dickey had been arrested and booked, finally, sometime close to six-thirty A.M. (time is very important in this tale). He called home and got his wife. His wife

called their lawyer. Lawyer said he could take care of things—
Dickey wouldn't even lose his license, but he would have to
take a special Drivers' Ed. course. But Lawyer wanted to
impress the seriousness of all this on Dickey, so he said he
would wait until *after* breakfast to bail out Big Jim. Breakfast, a particularly repellent meal at the jail, was served at
seven A.M. Dickey was out and on the way home by seven-
thirty A.M.

Now, to appreciate the rest of this, you have to know that
one of the things we, his fans, most admire about Big Jim is
that he is never daunted. Not ever. Not yet. So anyway, after
a while, couple of weeks, Ben Greer returns to South Carolina and pretty soon makes a courtesy call on his old teacher
and buddy Jim Dickey. Jim is real glad to see him, breaks
out a bottle of bourbon. And they have a few while catching
up on this and that. Dickey doesn't tell the story of the night
he hit the tree. But he does tell a bunch of stories that begin:
"Ben, when I was in prison . . ." And he gets quite excited
talking about the need for prison reform and how he and
Charles Colson and maybe Clifford Irving are going to form
a committee dedicated to prison reform. While all this is going
on, Ben notices an expensive notebook on the coffee table.
Notebook is labeled: The Prison Poems of James Dickey.

Then all of a sudden Dickey goes into a long story about
how he was once a Trusty in prison, with the run of the
place, and how one day he went into the empty room where
the electric chair is kept. Sat in it. Strapped one arm in place.
Sat there and imagined what it would be like to be electro-
cuted. Very moving scene.

Only trouble was that it comes directly out of Ben Greer's
first novel—*Slammer*. Ben is a real nice, polite Southern boy,
but this was going too far, taking his own story almost word

for word. "Damn it, Jim!" Ben burst out. "There isn't any electric chair in the Columbia city drunk tank!" Dickey blinked briefly, sipped his bourbon, but kept a poker face. Never daunted.

"Ben," he said quietly, "it's a *very small* electric chair. A lot of people don't even know it's there."

Ever since then, we, the fans, have pictured Big Jim sitting on a little bitty electric chair, about the size of a potty chair, a very low-voltage model that would take a week and a half to kill you.

University of Michigan
(1979–1980, 1982–1984)

Wonderful Pen
(A Snapshot)
When I bought this wonderful pen this morning,
at Ulrich's on South University in Ann Arbor,
the lady escorted me personally to the checkout counter,
maybe because I might try to sneak out without paying
but also because it was clearly a kind of an occasion
for me and for her and (I guess) for the store.
After all, how often does someone just walk in here
and ask for and pay cash for a $185 fountain pen?

The lady tells the girl at the cash register
what the pen costs and that I get a faculty discount
of 10 percent. Casually, then, I peel off and plunk down
four $50-bills, poor old U. S. Grant on the front of each.
It is payday, and I am feeling good, feeling fine.
I have been saving a long time for this stubby black
    Mont Blanc

with its bright gold nib that is sure to teach me some
   golden words.
I smile. Girl glares back her altogether savage
   disapproval.

"Jesus Christ!" she exclaims. "People are starving in
   places like Bangladesh!
They are killing each other with clubs in Uganda and
   Cambodia!
And you—I can't fucking *believe* it!—are spending a
   fortune
on a fountain pen! What can you possibly *do* with a pen
   like that?"
Saddened, embarrassed, but refusing to feel guilty, what
   can I say?
"Lady, this pen takes moving pictures; it records human
   voices and
if you stick it all the way up your ass, you'll find that
   you can sing
more sweet songs than a canary or a Georgia
   mockingbird."

VMI
(1982)

Only one semester there in beautiful Lexington in the
Shenandoah Valley with, all around, every which way the
theatrical presence of the Blue Ridge Mountains.

Not a heavy-duty intellectual atmosphere at the time,
but very nice people and very comfortable quarters in a
nineteenth-century frame house with lovely porches, facing
the parade grounds (full-dress parade every Friday), with a
steep hill falling away behind the row of houses.

Nice kids, by and large, too. Mostly working-class kids, a good many black, aiming at a commission and a career in the service. A few pale and vaguely decadent (you could spot them at a hundred yards) descendants of early alumni, fourth- and fifth-generation students from old Virginia families.

The routine, the bugles and whistles, the shouts and commands, the marching to and from class, the gray uniforms, and the glinting brass took me back, way back.

Some funny things happened, to be sure. My so-called creative writing class was almost entirely made up of football players. They mostly wrote odd little poems full of imagery that would have delighted Dr. Freud by confirming his theories. We would cover the day's crop of poems in, say, half an hour, then spend the rest of the period talking football. They knew I had played and coached in kinder, gentler times—only no face masks, guys; lots of missing teeth and broken noses—and that I was a sucker for the subject.

When they were getting ready to play Virginia over in Charlottesville, one of the guys, I think his name was Pappas but can't be sure, worked out a system with me. Pappas was a wonderful athlete. He could have played anywhere in America and at a number of positions. He was just a very good football player, very cool and cocky, sure of himself and not greatly impressed with opposing players even when, as in the case of Virginia, they were playing some big-time football.

Of course, this is always true. A place like VMI will have maybe half a dozen ball players who could play for anybody. Not enough to win or to withstand the attrition of a team with thirty or forty first-rate people, but enough, anyway, to play well against them for quite a while. Add to that the fact that all of the VMI players, if only because of the physical rigor of their daily lives, were in superb physical condition, better on average than any team they played. And so that Saturday they played pretty well against UVa until the fourth quarter, when they faded. I think VMI was even ahead for a while in the second quarter.

Anyway, Pappas, knowing that I was going to be sitting with old buddies on the Virginia side of Scott Stadium, worked out a set of signals for me. You see, Pappas, being Mr. Cool, brought in the plays from the coach to the huddle. So the coach would call the play and Pappas would signal me what the play was going to be even before he made it onto the field and into the huddle.

Thus I knew what the VMI play was going to be before the quarterback (who was also my student) did.

No harm done. I looked pretty good, prescient you might say, to my faculty buddies from UVa. I would say something like: "Well, I guess they'll throw a pass this time."

"On *first* down?"

"Why not?"

The code we had was unique. But scouts for other teams, particularly Virginia Tech, which was to play VMI the following week, couldn't know that. I've often wondered if they noticed (if not, they *should* have) that every time Pappas tapped the top of his helmet they passed. I like to think they broke the code, figured it out, and were all ready for it next Saturday. To no purpose. It was used once and once only. . . .

But that is not *the* VMI anecdote. The VMI anecdote is about Robert Coover, that highly regarded, much-praised metafictionist, that postmodern, postindustrial, quasi-surrealist fabulator. Twice I have followed in the footsteps of Mr. Coover, once at Princeton, where I was assigned his old office, still containing many of his books and pictures. Which, over several years, I came to enjoy. And at VMI, where he had been the visiting writer the year before.

When I arrived, they asked me if I would like to have the same office he had used. I said any old office would do. They went on to say that the office he had chosen was in the back of the building, quiet and isolated from everything else.

"I guess he likes a quiet place to work," I ventured.

Probably, they allowed, but that wasn't really it, not what it was really all about. The whole thing was (according to the VMI English faculty) that Coover was deeply disturbed by the loud and constant hazing of the "rats," the new cadets. It was a moral issue with him, they told me. So he asked for and received a remote office where he couldn't hear the shouts and cries and whispers and whimpers even if he had wanted to.

True or not?

I don't know. Don't care. But it strikes me as a wonderful symbol for a whole generation of 1960s holier-than-thou literati. You express your moral disapproval of something or other (receiving, of course, full credit and plenty of points for your sensitivity and superior ethical standards) while turning your back to it and moving away to a safe distance.

Preferring even hazing to hypocrisy, I thanked them kindly and asked for an office where the noise and clamor of the world (its raw and wonderful music) could constantly remind me that I am alive and in it until the day I die.

Unwritten Stories and Untold Tales

From a goat with a face like a Jew
I learned by heart the ancient wail,
the lament of all living things.
　　　—Umberto Saba, "Goat"

The whole thing is—always was, I guess, but it's clear enough to me now, plainly undeniable—that I can never live long enough to write a lot of the stories I have had in mind for a long time. No way.

Of course, some of them have been preempted, used up by others, the general subjects, anyway. Here are a couple or three.

Take, for example, the heartbreak of psoriasis. I have it (not as badly as it might be, thank God). But so do John Updike, Gordon Lish, and Nicholson Baker. And they have all written about it in some detail, for better or worse. To be sure, something like one out of four or five white Americans has at least a touch of psoriasis, so it is common enough. Still, I waited too long. I am older than all of those writers and should have written anything I had to say on the subject long ago.

Too late now.

Except there is one little anecdote I can't help retailing here and now. Set in the early 1960s at the University of Virginia, where I was first (more or less) diagnosed.

What happened was that quite suddenly I was covered with lesions and scales, head to toe. Like overnight. Went to see my doctor, a fine fellow all around, who said, "Beats me." And sent me to see the head of dermatology at the university hospital. Who checked this and that and then discovered, to his considerable pleasure, that I was suffering from a serious strep throat. He was very pleased because, it seemed, I was the living proof of some kind of a hypothesis he had allowed himself in a recent article. It was an article that he had required all of his students to read.

He thereupon proposed to me that if I were willing to submit to an examination by his dermatology class, he would, in return, give me free treatment for my condition. It didn't sound too difficult. I was to sit bare-ass in an examining room and allow his students, one at a time, to come in and, briefly, examine me. I was to answer any questions they elected to ask me, honestly and fully, but I was not to volunteer any information or to make any suggestions.

Seemed easy enough. Why not? It's no fun to be a piece of meat, especially an unhealthy one, in the presence of a lot of strangers. But it wasn't exactly the first time. I reckoned I could stand it if they could.

Nobody asked about my throat or even looked at it. One by one they looked at me, took some notes, and left. Finally the last of them was gone, and I had just started to get dressed when a kid came charging into the room. His clothes were rumpled and his white jacket was stained and dirty. He was unshaven, red-eyed.

"Christ, do I have a hangover!" he said. He sat down in the chair I had vacated. Lit a cigarette with slightly trembling fingers.

"What the fuck am I supposed to do with you?" he asked.

"Check my throat," I said, opening wide.

I would like to think (I never asked) he was the only one in class to guess and get the assignment right. I like to think he went on to a successful and lucrative career in dermatology. What harm could that be? What harm could he do?

Later the professor invited me into his office to discuss my free treatment.

"What we have here is either psoriasis or parapsoriasis, one or the other, I think," he said. "Not that it matters a whole lot, because the treatment is the same."

He suggested some medication that ought to calm things down a little. If it didn't work, there would be other choices.

"It's almost summer and that's a good time for these skin problems," he allowed. "Try sunbathing. Sun could help your condition a lot. On the other hand, sun can sometimes aggravate it. So be careful.

"Salt water is sometimes very helpful," he continued. "Go to the beach when you can. Be careful, though, because sometimes salt water makes it a lot worse. . . ."

And so it went. Maybe this will help you get well. But maybe it will make it worse. Finally the distinguished professor of dermatology (actually a classmate of mine from Princeton, otherwise I would not have dared to speak up to a *doctor*) paused and looked at me, smiling. Tall, lean, very good-looking fellow. Very nice, smooth skin, now that I noticed.

"Truth is," I heard myself saying, "you don't know a hell of a lot about this, do you?"

He flicked an inner switch and the smile vanished.

"No," he said. "I don't. But, then, I don't *have* it, either, do I?"

The look he offered me was pure disgust. And at that moment and ever after I understood how they, doctors, feel about us with our disgusting conditions, our nasty symptoms, our contemptible diseases. They will work, most of them and to the best of their knowledge and abilities, to heal us, their patients. But, heart of hearts, what they truly love is good health and physical beauty.

Serves them right, doesn't it, that they are condemned by vocation to deal daily with the sick, the hurt, the lame, the losers. They have elected a Christlike profession, if you forget about the abundant rewards they are given here and now, in this world if not the next.

The Tanks

When William Styron published *The Long March,* I could have done a Sufi dervish dance and died on the spot. Truth is, it was a fine, strong, clean piece of work. One of his very best, maybe *the* best, though I have always liked *Set This House on Fire* because it is opulent and extravagant in both its style and substance and he tries more. I have to confess, too, that I wanted to like *Set This House on Fire* because the critics and reviewers had thumped it pretty good. Styron the public figure (I don't know the "real" one, the flesh-and-blood Styron; I've seen him in action a couple of times and, of course, on

the tube, and the first impression I got was verbal; the words
pompous and *pontifical* lit up like neon in my mental dictionary, but I am leery of the truth of my first impressions)
struck me as the kind of guy who probably read his own
press clippings and then memorized all the good ones. Since
he had been so eloquently and elegantly praised for the art of
Lie Down in Darkness, he would at least be somewhat inclined
to take the opinions of critics and reviewers seriously, wouldn't
he?

It was a chuckle, anyway. In the groves of academe, where
I was stuck earning a living (briefly, briefly, to be sure; sooner
rather than later some kind of a break or a breakthrough
would set me free to be a real, full-time writer—wouldn't
it?), I could always raise an eyebrow or two by saying, when
the right occasion arose, that my two favorite Hemingway
novels were *To Have and Have Not* and *Across the River and
into the Trees,* that *A Fable* was the Faulkner novel I admired
most. Moving to nearer time, I would boldly celebrate, say,
James Jones's *Some Came Running,* Norman Mailer's *The Deer
Park,* and, of course, *Set This House on Fire.*

I really liked *The Long March,* even though it was spooky
how it shadowed a thing that had happened to me that I had
wanted to write about. Both stories take place during the
time of the Korean War and both take place in the United
States. Both involve reservists called to active duty and training. Both begin with an act of violence. In Styron's story some
mortar rounds fall short of target and kill some marines. The
story I was going to write commences, just as it did in real
life, with a tank accidentally driving over some sleeping soldiers. A tank suddenly and hugely looming out of dawn mist
and half-light is truly a terrifying shape. I don't know if those
guys woke up enough in their sleeping bags to see what was

fixing to crush and kill them (a tank is so noisy; they must have heard it, but they had been up all night on some kind of training exercise), but if they did see it, the last thing they saw in this world was monstrous.

That's where I wanted to begin, with the sudden deafening noise of tank engines and treads, then with the view of the soldiers zipped into their sleeping bags as the dark, cold, enormous shape of the tank appears above them and plows through the little bivouac.

Somebody among them must escape. Bound to.

I would open with noise in misty dark. Then the tank as seen by the soldiers. One of whom, shouting to no purpose against the roaring engine, scrabbles and writhes his way to escape and looks back at the wide treadmarks in the soft earth where he has just been. Leave him there weeping and gagging as other men from all around come running.

Cut away to us, our outfit, a mile or so away from the scene.

We don't hear or know anything yet. We will hear about it later. At the end of our day. But it will haunt us, shadow us all day long.

We are a field artillery battalion of an under-strength U.S. Army Reserve division. We are doing two weeks of summer training at Camp Drum near Watertown, New York. There are two divisions training here, ourselves and the New Jersey National Guard. I think that they were the Eighty-eighth Division. The bad scene with the tanks and one tank driving right over sleeping soldiers involved troops from the National Guard.

(Guess who was the commanding officer of that division at that time. General Schwarzkopf, the *father* of Stormin' Norman. And guess where Stormin' Norman's daddy went that summer. Answer: Iran. Look it up some time.)

In those days both the reserve and the National Guard were still chiefly composed of veterans of World War II and (already) Korea. Most everybody did it for the money and the benefits. At least that's what they all said. It wasn't, yet, a ticket to avoid full-time active duty. Joining the reserve or the National Guard didn't spare you anything in those days.

I was just back from a couple of years of active duty overseas in Trieste and Austria. I was a married graduate student at Princeton and I needed the money, needed every nickel and dime I could get. I had come out of the army as a sergeant first class, a nice swaggering kind of rank. Together with the next rank, master sergeant, it was better than being anything else except maybe a field-grade officer.

We met in an armory near Trenton, New Jersey, one night a week (drawing a full day's pay for those two hours) and for two weeks of summer training.

We were a pretty good outfit. Everybody had seen service overseas. A lot of them, especially old-timers from World War II, had logged a lot of combat hours. We had one sergeant who had been captured by the Krauts at Kasserine Pass. Our first sergeant had been bayoneted by a Jap and lived to tell the tale and to show a huge, pink, swollen scar, chest and back, in the shower.

The old guys weren't much for spit and polish, but they knew everything that could ever be known about and done with our basic weapon—the 105-millimeter howitzer.

Styron's story, as I recall it, centers on two young marine infantry lieutenants and their commanding officer, who is some kind of a shithead. There isn't much sense of the outfit from their point of view. A couple of candy-ass second lieutenants. What do they know about anything?

When we got up that day, had reveille and breakfast in the field, we found out what was scheduled for the day. A speed march. We had been firing our howitzers on the range for a few days. Now we were going back to camp. Instead of riding back in trucks we were going to hike it back. *(Hump* is the Vietnam word for it and I guess is more accurately poetic than *hike.)* I seem to remember hearing some of the officers arguing among themselves at breakfast. I was hunkered down blowing on my canteen cup, breathing the sweet steam of fresh coffee and waiting for my cup to cool, when I heard them, nearby and oblivious to me, complaining about the speed march. Seems it was the colonel's idea. Or, anyway, somebody had dared him or challenged him and he took the dare.

The fuck did I care? I was young and strong, in good shape, still in my twenties. Had done this kind of thing many times, within months of here and now. I was able and ready. I had in my pack a pair of women's nylon panties. Nothing better to wear for a speed march. Regular underwear got creased and snarled up and would chafe and rub blisters. And I never went anywhere, especially in the field, without my little can of foot powder and a thin, tight pair of nylon socks to wear underneath the heavy GI socks for a hike.

There may have been other tricks of the trade (I know I discarded everything except essential equipment so my load would be as light as I could make it), but I can't remember them.

When I came to write the story I would have to make something out of myself as a character. Not something nice. There would be this guy, see, much like myself, a sergeant first class just back from active duty overseas. He would have earned his stripes at a leadership school. He would be what we used to call *sharp*. He would know a lot of things. He would be highly and quietly contemptuous of all the old-timers and their old wars and wounds. He would be especially contemptuous of the red-haired first sergeant with the bayonet scar. That contempt would be, he thinks, because the first sergeant is so soft and easygoing. A pussy is what our sergeant first class would classify him. Never out loud, of course, and never by any sign or twitch on his well-trained poker face. Truth is, the first sergeant likes him, thinks he is a good soldier and a good guy. Which only adds more coals to the younger man's contempt.

What the younger man will not admit to himself is that the real source of his contempt for the first sergeant is rivalry. He wants to be first sergeant of the battery. Deeper yet, he would like to have been wounded, himself. Nothing like those ugly bayonet scars, but some nice little nick he could show in the shower or maybe show off to some girl when the time came.

Our real colonel, the battalion commander, was a great guy and one of the finest officers I ever served under. He was a big, tall, good-looking guy, going to fat now, but impressive. Black hair and a big smile. He treated all his subordinates with respect and with trust. The latter is a very rare thing in the army or any other hierarchical or corporate organization. You can't trust too many people too much because they may let you down and then you are in more trouble than they are. But the colonel, whose name has now gone from me for good, could take the heat. The buck stopped with him. He was the same with us regardless of the pressure on him. Same in success or adversity. A whole man and a fearless one, really.

My young sergeant first class might not, probably *would* not, appreciate him for what he was (though I think he would have learned enough about leadership to sense that the colonel is a genuine leader; he might even envy that), but he would, at least at the outset, respect him and want to win his notice and approval.

Our colonel, the real one, the big guy, was a heavy boozer. I could tell after a mile in the hot sun that he would never make it. He didn't seem to know that. He insisted on *leading* the batallion. Up front about ten yards or so. Sure, he didn't have to carry a field pack or anything extra except his steel helmet and his M-2 carbine. But there was a lot of him and he really was not in shape for it. A mile or so and his tight coveralls (he wore World War II coveralls, zipped up the front, not fatigues like the rest of us) were wet and soaking with his sweat. After another mile or so he was bright red. Couple more miles and he turned purple, a dark, grapey purple color. And he was breathing hard. But he kept moving and grinning, leading the pack, which was beginning to stagger and stretch out behind him. Old-timers finding out the hard way that they couldn't hack it anymore. Or, anyway, giving up before they had to learn any bad lessons about themselves.

He was good about breaks. Ten minutes every hour.

Everybody sprawled out like dropped rag dolls at roadside. Himself not taking a break, but moving up and down the line, encouraging the guys, calling for the medics to get a move on if somebody had acquired bad blisters.

I was feeling okay. No way you aren't tired and muscle-weary. But you are still young and blessed with quick recovery.

During the break I sat by the road and watched the colonel, wondering if he would make it. Guessing that he would not.

My sergeant first class will come to the same conclusion, but with very mixed feelings. He will be somebody who is always made uncomfortable by the clash of contradictory feelings but is nevertheless often possessed by them. His ideal will be pure and simple feeling, single-mindedness. But mostly he will be more complicated than he wants to be. Pity is beyond him, of course. That would be simple enough, but contemptible. And, no denying it, there is always some pleasure in observing someone with power and authority failing, fucking up. At the same time, because he thinks the colonel likes him, thinks (and hopes) the colonel can see him for what he really is and can be—a likely choice for first sergeant—he wants the colonel's authority, credibility, self-respect to be undiminished. What good would it do to have a big loser on your side?

He will sit by the side of the road and watch the purple-faced, sweaty, grinning, brave old colonel in his tight coveralls and will want to warn him. To look after him. To make sure the colonel makes it all the way.

What if the old fart falls over dead?

I forget what happens in the middle of the Styron story. Details are long gone. I do remember being impressed that the writing and the accumulation of details are so good that the march back to base assumes an urgency, some real suspense.

That is the whole line of any march story, whether it's a speed march or a forty-year trek in the wilderness. There is a destination. There are many difficulties (demons and dragons, outer and inner) to overcome before arriving at the final destination.

Styron's two lieutenants do, indeed, make it back, more or less in one piece, to the bachelor officers' quarters.

So did our outfit. So did the colonel. He led us first to last. We ended up in a little shady grove of trees not far from our barracks. Took off packs and helmets. Propped our weapons, M-1s and carbines, on the packs or against tree trunks. Lay there in the hot shade, breathing hard at the very end, sweat turning the dust on our faces and bodies into a thin, muddy coat.

It was like a little island in the middle of nowhere. Like we were survivors of a shipwreck, tossed up on shore in the shade there.

I had my eyes on the colonel. Who finally allowed himself to sit down, back firm against the trunk of a pine tree. Nobody was watching him except me. Very slowly, gingerly, he began to unlace and remove his combat boots. I noticed his hands were shaking a little, his fingers trembling. When the first boot was unbuckled and unlaced he very slowly, carefully eased it off his foot. Held the foot lightly in both hands and bent close to look at it. I could see that the soles were bloody and had soaked through his regulation GI socks. Blisters, and they had broken and bled and he had walked (how many miles?), leading the battalion all the way home on bloody feet.

And now I think for the first time how the pain of his bloody feet came alive and swept over him. He knew what had happened and what he had done and the pride went out of him like a long sigh.

I saw his large jowly face, a hurt moan beneath the gray and black of his thick, close-cropped hair, begin to change. As if it were wax in heat. Too close to flame. Begin to change and melt.

That colonel (and I knew it and so would my character) had been a captain and a battery commander in the Battle of the Bulge. Had a battery of 155-millimeter howitzers and they were firing support at a distant and unseen enemy when suddenly a bunch of Kraut Tiger tanks came barreling into the battery area. Came out of nowhere from all sides. Pure killing machines killing everything moving. Killed most of the battery and wounded the captain. Desperately wounded, unable to move, he somehow lived to see the tanks drive over his men, treads gorging mud a few feet from himself.

In his hurt and stricken face there at the end of our speed march I could tell he was suddenly alive in that old nightmare again. I could see and feel all of it as vividly as if I had been there and could remember it, too.

And then suddenly he was shouting at the top of a cracked, hoarse voice, begging for one of the medics to come quick. To please come. To help him. Please . . . !

Falling completely apart at the tag end after holding himself and all the rest of it together for so long. Suddenly now becoming an old man in pain and surprise beyond all bearing.

I could not look anymore. Turned away from him. Tried to busy myself with my own sore feet and stiff legs.

In the story I was someday going to write (and never did until this moment) my sergeant first class would not, does not turn away. He looks directly into the pain-riddled eyes of his colonel. Both of them sharing now the vision that has haunted the edges of consciousness all day—those great dark shapes, towering and terrible in vision, of the tanks, rearing and lunging out of the woods and brush, bringing death to those sleeping soldiers, this selfsame day. For a moment they can share this vision, can share this death.

The sergeant first class is possessed by mixed feelings still, as always. But one of them, one of those feelings, anyway, is very close to the stab and thrust of love. He has forgotten the first sergeant, his imaginary rival, and his ugly bayonet scar. Probably the first sergeant did not even finish the march. Now it is the colonel my character loves and envies and admires with mixed feelings. One of those feelings takes the form of a wish. Wishing that he, the young man, could somehow take on himself all of the colonel's pain and dismay, and his wealth of terrible memory, all of it, and thereby leave the old man his pride.

Another Separate Peace

An empty street. Gray, wintry day. Bare, wind-picked trees. A dead leaf or two scuttling with the breeze. Old houses, set well back from the curbless street, most needing a coat of paint and other basic upkeep. Nothing moving except the occasional leaf and the sway of white wood smoke from some of the chimneys.

Suddenly a dog barks. Barks again at something we cannot hear.

At this point the black woman appears in the street. Pulling a little red wagon behind her. She has a stick that must be a kind of cane. She is all wrapped up in shabby and raggedy layers of wool clothing. Shy as an animal, a doe, though in fact only we are looking at her. And we are not there except in and through these words. Junk in the red wagon. Like what we now call a "bag lady." Closer, we see by her face and her hair that she is old, very old, old beyond telling or remembering.

Dog barks again.

Now we, too, hear something. As the ancient black woman pauses close by the protection of a blue spruce tree. She cocks her head like a robin. Listens.

We hear a military drum beat. Steady. Then a shrill whistle, a drum roll, and a military band suddenly playing, blasting the chill, gray air. Band is playing "Onward Christian Soldiers."

Cut to color guard leading the band. Which in turn is leading the battalion of cadets from the Sewanee Military Academy. Up the middle of the street, rounding a curve. Now in the same frame and shot with the black woman.

The cadets are all wearing their heavy, gray wool, full-length overcoats, scarlet capes folded back and clipped into place, double row of brass buttons gleaming. Black shoes, traditional gray uniforms, garrison caps set two fingers over the eyes. Officers with drawn sabers and Sam Brown belts. Color guards armed with their beautiful M1903 A3 Springfield rifles. Flags, the American and the school flag, snapping in a sudden gust of wind.

The old black woman, holding onto the handle of her child's wagon, cringing a little into the space of the blue spruce, watches them march by.

Something like a sly, toothless smile on her lips.

Onward, Christian soldiers.

We are in Sewanee, Tennessee, on the mountain, on the ten-thousand-acre domain of the University of the South. It is 1944, year of World War II. No end of that war in sight.

The cadets are marching to church, to the chapel of the university with its high nave, its stained-glass windows, its fading Confederate battle flags. Marching to church as they do every Sunday, Gentile and Jew, Protestant and Catholic, each and all Episcopalians for today, like it or not.

A block more and the band moves onto the lawn before the church, still playing as the cadets, platoon after platoon, march inside, whipping off their garrison caps as they enter.

Behind them the black woman is moving again about her own business. She has seen all this before, many times. Born into slavery, she can vaguely remember other gray soldiers (not so fine in their uniforms, all raggedy, in fact, and many of them about the same age as these boys), and blue ones, too, on horses on this street during that other war. Which changed her life a little. For better and for worse.

That was the time and place and situation for a story I wanted to write, was going to write, might still write if I live a little longer than I'm supposed to. Sat on it and pondered it too long. For I really just began to feel and conceive it as a story to be told way back then, right while it was happening. I had no serious plans to be a writer. Not yet. But I often thought about how I could shape and twist and design a story out of what was happening to me and around me. I kept thinking, then and later, that something might well be made out of those wartime high-school years spent in Sewanee, that lonesome, isolated, beautiful, and changeless mountain village.

John Knowles, of course, did his version, World War II seen and felt and experienced at a New England prep school (Exeter).

For what it was worth, like Styron's *The Long March,* the subject belonged to him. Still does, I suppose, though I think the ambience of a military school and the isolation and the Southernness of things—the haunting sense and awareness of defeat—for our generation was the last that could claim flesh-and-bones contact with the veterans of that Civil War and, too, some of the former slaves like that ancient, wizened woman on the mountain (I sometimes imagined she may have brooded, with her sly, shy smile, over the troops marching to Waterloo and maybe even Thermopylae); those battle flags lining both sides of the long nave of the university chapel, now gone, I am told, replaced by entirely peaceful and mostly meaningless and cheerful banners by our trendy Episcopalian church, ever eager not to offend anyone, real or imaginary, except their fellow Episcopalians.

My story would have its share of sex and violence. A cadet, probably the protagonist, loses his virginity in a pew of that same chapel one dark, wintry night. As for violence, it was continual and always expected from reveille to taps and afterward. I remember some terrific fistfights and wrestling in the soap-slick showers and have always thought such a scene might manage to capture not only the heart-pounding joy of uninhibited violence, but also the vague yet strenuous element of homoeroticism. It was real and unspoken (unspeakable) and very dangerous. Younger boys, inevitably, developed "crushes" on the older ones. Precarious as these crushes might be, they are, I suppose, one way to learn how to love another human being. It would have to be there.

So would murderous hatred, part of the military experience exacerbated by all the furies of adolescence.

There are many caves in the deep woods of the mountain. Some are tricky and difficult, must be entered and left by complex ways and means. Sometimes a cadet gets trapped in one of those caves and has to be rescued. What if, I found myself thinking even as with a couple of buddies I climbed in and out of caves, what if someone deliberately arranged it so that an enemy was trapped in one of those caves? Then no one told about it. Days would pass. The missing kid would be believed to be AWOL, a runaway. There were always a few who vanished in the middle of the night.

There would be murder here as there was murder all over the world. It would all be part of the war. The war they were all going to anyway, they believed.

I tried to imagine the one boy (myself) killing the other

one (myself as well) out of love and hate and fury. And how it would be. Guessed then that he, the killer, would be all right, in control of himself, able to rationalize and dissemble even to himself *so long as it was not only possible but highly likely that he was soon enough going to war.* He would be ready to die, convinced that his readiness to die (whether he was killed or not) would be a full and sufficient payment for whatever happened (he could no longer remember clearly) in the cave to the other boy he loved and hated.

The atomic bomb, which nobody had even imagined, except maybe Einstein, and the sudden end of the war, which, though desirable, was unbelievable, would, as I pictured it, break him. When he tried to confess his crime, he would not be believed, for lots of good reasons, and would be taken to be mad.

So, in a sense, he would become a casualty of the war as much as if he had gone to it and been killed or wounded in fact.

Sometimes I still think about these things as if they had really happened. I have reached no conclusion yet. Which is why I tell myself I can never write it, even though I know full well that the only way to arrive at some kind of conclusion is to write my way there and back.

Under
Two Flags

1.

Picture this, if you will. Kissimmee, Florida, in the heart of the Great Depression. A small, shabby little place. Then, blessed with the rich shade of live oaks and so offering a few moments of shadowy respite from the heat and dust and glare all around for miles. Walt Disney World is near there now, and the old place looks pretty, and pretty much like every place else. But it was a cow town then, a hard, tough place where life was hard and tough and had turned bitter for many decent people.

It is evening then and there. A quiet time. Streetlights coming on. People in their houses finishing the supper dishes or sitting outside on the front porch. Or maybe inside, looking at and listening to the radio. Some of them will be going downtown to the picture show. To Bank Night.

We, our family, have piled into our old car, my mother and my father and the children and maybe a friend or two, and gone into town to the drugstore for an ice-cream cone.

My father parks the car in front and we go inside to sit on tall swivel chairs at the counter, eating our ice-cream cones and enjoying the cool breeze from the slow-paddling overhead fans.

We are sitting there in a row when the young policeman walks in. Try as I will now, I can't remember his name anymore. Only that he was very young—every year now he seems, like the stone and bronze soldiers of public monuments, to grow younger and younger. He was young, and my mother, who was a teacher then, had taught him in high school. Politely, he greeted her first. After which he seemed, for a moment, a little awkward and embarrassed.

"Mr. Garrett," he said to my father, "I'm afraid I'm going to have to give you a red ticket."

(*Red ticket* was the generic name, in those days, for a traffic ticket.)

"Really?" my father said, still licking at his ice-cream cone. "What for?"

"Well, sir, your taillights aren't working."

"That's funny," he said. "They were working just fine when we came down here."

"Well, sir, they sure don't work now."

My father turned around on his chair and looked into the young man's eyes. I could hear the whispery whish and squeech of the fans.

"All right," my father said at last. "Let's go outside and have a look."

2.

Let us leave this scene, for the moment, as the policeman and my father and mother and all of us, clutching our precious ice-cream cones, troop outside to look at our car. We'll be back there a little later.

Let us dissolve through time and space back to the late 1860s and a large if somewhat rundown house on a quiet street in a town in Georgia. I am not at all sure now which town it may have been. Because when I heard about this I wasn't listening as closely and carefully as I might have and now wish that I had been. Because I was not listening, never really planning to incorporate this story into any pattern of my life, I am weak on the details (large and small), some of those the essential specifics that allow the spirit its freedom to give life. But, as you will see, my ignorance is part of the story. I can tell you this much. The town might have been, almost had to be, Perry, Georgia. Or maybe Macon or Way-cross. No matter. It was one of those places. The house, already old then, was crowded and full of life. First of all, there were the handful of junior officers, Union officers who were, with all the lawful force of the recently suspended Fourth Amendment to the Constitution, being billeted there. And there were women, a few older women and several young women, aunts and cousins, living together in the one place left standing and belonging to them—in the aftermath of the Civil War. The older women were glad to have the Union officers present, grateful for the protection and the rent and the rations that came with them. To an extent, always allowing that they had been, after all, the enemy, the older women mothered them and looked after them. They were, to be sure, about the same age as their own sons and kinfolk who had not come home. To the inexperienced young women, no more than girls, these aliens in blue uniforms were still the enemy. Beneath notice, if not contempt.

When everyone, women and officers, sat down at the great

round dining-room table for midday dinner, it was, as you can imagine, a somewhat strained occasion at which the noises of cutlery and china were often more emphatic than any kind of sustained talk, louder than human voices.

Sometimes the officers tried to tease the young women into an exchange of conversation. But the girls stared at their plates, or else coolly at something eight hundred yards away, and allowed the Yankees only the indulgence of a few mumbled monosyllables.

The ranking matriarch—whose name would have been Dorothy or Priscilla or Emily, I believe—spoke privately to her daughters and nieces. To no avail. She also spoke to the ranking young officer, an infantry captain from Boston. Or was it Illinois? Anyway, he proved to be tactful and understanding. And more than a little amused. He told her that he had a plan in mind to ease the tension somewhat, though he did not share with her (yet) what it might be.

3.

The most obvious division of all older American families is, of course, the Civil War. To think and talk about the family under two flags, we simply cannot avoid thinking and talking about the great house divided, a nation divided and, as it happened, dismembered by its division. Like so many old American families, mine fought on both sides. And, in truth, those on the same side were often very far apart. For example, one Confederate soldier in our family, a man I knew in fact and flesh, one who had experienced more than his share of the most brutal and bloody combat of the war, was, until the day the war actually commenced, a dedicated and outspoken Abolitionist.

I am speaking and thinking here and now of a family that was then in the White Tribe. I say *was* because many of the newest and youngest generation of the family have married well outside the Tribe and its close kinship and affiliations. This nation's recently self-conscious awareness of plurality and diversity is already our own, has been for a while. The latest generation is a kind of representative rainbow coalition of wide ethnic and even racial diversity in a geographically far-flung family. There are now blacks and Orientals who bear our various family names and are part of its continuing history. But then, in those lost days, it was much more limited and can honestly be called part of the White Tribe. And when I speak of this family as a part of that tribe, I do so with full awareness that this is only one part of a much wider and deeper and more complex history of the nation. A history that, to be sure, profoundly involves other tribes, and especially Native Americans and African Americans.

One of the things I was trained in during my army days and years was the art and craft of land mines, booby traps, and demolition. It was terrifying and interesting stuff, and I wish I could digress, pausing here to tell you more about it, how it was, especially since the world of high-tech terrorism that we now much inhabit makes that simpler world seem to be ancient history. But the reason I mention this is to say that I know very well that I am already moving through a kind of mine field. I intend to be careful, very careful. I am sure that you understand that some of the topics I must touch upon can be highly explosive, more dangerous than entertaining or charming. So be it. I am not appealing for votes or for love. My family loves me and that is more than enough. And I have to argue that any kind of search for the truth—especially in our highly politicized and urgently cautious intellectual scene—conducted seriously and honestly is very much like the business of trying to clear a safe pathway through a mine field.

Is it worth the danger and the effort?

Here I cite Thomas Jefferson's words carved in stone over a doorway at Cabell Hall at the University of Virginia, words that I see every day and have to think about even though I do not see any firm evidence that these words have fully registered upon the majority of my involuntary colleagues in the English department. Anyway, Jefferson wrote: "Here we are not afraid to follow Truth wherever it may lead nor to tolerate any error so long as reason is left free to combat it."

Consider that these words are as radical now as they were then.

I begin with the two flags of the Civil War, not only and merely because our family was haunted by it, but also because it is my best judgment that very little of the life of our family now, or many aspects of life in the new America, could ever have come to pass without the Civil War. Not just the results of that war, victory and defeat, but the war itself.

In spite of growing and towering mountains, huge slag piles of factual history and many kinds and forms of poetry and fiction, and even the wonders of television, it is still very difficult to imagine the Civil War accurately and honestly. True, the issues and the results, both obvious and hidden, the texts and the subtexts have been ceaselessly explored and investigated and analyzed by scholars and thinkers and artists. And it is a situation not without a certain irony in this sense: the twentieth century is the vantage point from which all of us have to view our American past, and the twentieth century has been primarily noteworthy as an age of incredibly bloody and uninterrupted warfare. War and its inevitable complement of atrocities are and have been the predominant experiences of this, our century. So one might reasonably think, might expect, might even hope, that we have at least learned some things about the nature of warfare and have come to understand it better. And in one sense we have. For example, we all seem to know well enough by now that in war the issues and causes, good or evil, are of meaning and value only for recruiting purposes as well as to ease (somewhat) the hearts and minds of the folks at home. Surely by now no honest soldier can admit to entertaining the idea that the good guys, the ones on the "right" and the "just" side, are enabled to fight any better or more fiercely and bravely or successfully than the bad guys. Any honest veteran, in a world of veterans, will have to tell you that history is purely and simply and always the victors' version of events. And that justice is whatever the victors say it is. True that issues and causes are, indeed, fought over and about, tested, but the people actually doing the fighting and dying, the warriors then, take their consolation and receive their inspiration elsewhere. Though it seems, also, to be true that when they are old and gray and full of dreams, the last lucky survivors begin to misremember it.

But sometimes not.

Here, for example, taken from Shelby Foote's masterpiece, his account in *The Civil War: A Narrative,* is one old Civil War veteran's memory of the war and a sense of its meaning to him: "I think that, as life is action and passion, it is required of a man that he should share the passion and action of his time at peril of being judged not to have lived." So said Oliver Wendell Holmes in Keene, New Hampshire, on the evening of 30 May 1884. "The generation that carried on the war has been set aside by its experience," he continued.

"Through our great good fortune, in our youth our hearts were touched with fire. It was given to us to learn at the outset that life is a profound and passionate thing. While we are permitted to scorn nothing but indifference, and do not pretend to undervalue the worldly rewards of ambition, we have seen with our own eyes, beyond and above the gold fields, the snowy heights of honor, and it is for us to bear the report to those who come after us."

That image of snow summons up cold and purity. And the only unsoilable purity of the Civil War lies in its combat history. All the rest, political and social, has been, inevitably, tainted and distorted. When the war was over, the union had been preserved, though we are, even now—and most likely always will be, at least so long as any union remains and endures—testing and trying to determine and to define whatever that preservation (and that union) may mean. The one thing that seems to have been settled once and for all, absolutely, is that slavery ended in the United States. Without the war it probably would not have ended anytime soon. It was the war that ended it. It is worth keeping in mind, always, that only the war, only a military victory, ended and could have ended slavery. A negotiated settlement, at any point (and there were serious negotiations, even very late), would have treated that issue, like any and all others, as negotiable. In England slavery could come to an end by legislation, by statute. In America it ended in the only way that it could have, by massive bloodshed.

(It remains worth remembering, too, that still, in various nations and places in the Third World, the custom of slavery, in various forms and disguised by various names, continues shamelessly.)

In one of my three favorite modern novels about the Civil

War, Stephen Becker's *When the War Is Over*—the other two
are Shelby Foote's *Shiloh* and Mary Lee Settle's *Know Nothing*—there is this very brief exchange between Jacob Courtney, a freed slave, and the central character, Captain Marius
Catto of the Union Army. The context is that Jacob is explaining to the captain the background of a young Confederate guerilla who has recently been taken prisoner:

> "So the boy always pretty much alone," Jacob went
> on. "Live off what he hunt and keep to the woods a
> lot. He don't even know what this war is all about."
>
> "Neither do I some days," Catto says.
>
> "About slavery, this war is. No doubt about that.
> About Jacob Courtney and his people."

The truth of the Civil War is one of the darkest secrets
of the American experience. We have come to know everything about it except how unbelievably terrible it was. In *The
Civil War* Foote gives us plenty of numbers to consider: "The
butcher's bill came to no less than 1,094,453 for both sides, in
and out of 10,000 military actions, including 76 full-scale battles, 310 engagements, 6,337 skirmishes and numerous sieges,
raids, expeditions, and the like. . . ." A little later, in simple
words that ought to be branded on flesh, he writes: "Approximately one out of ten able-bodied Northerners was dead or
incapacitated, while for the South it was one out of four,
including her noncombatant Negroes."

In other words, for the North the ratio of *military* casualties to population was worse than that of any nation in World
War I or World War II. For the South it was worse than
any historical example, ancient or modern, that Foote could
find, except, perhaps, for the Tai-Ping Rebellion in China,

for which no count was kept or ever made, but which cost many millions of lives.

The dark secret is, then, that the American Civil War was in a sense the worst war in modern history. Anywhere. Somehow, in spite of all the gleaned and recorded facts and all but a few (and these very recent) works of the imagination, the brute truth of this and all its complex implications have not been grasped.

How can such things be kept or, anyway, remain secret? With our open society and our enormously powerful and probing press, the so-called media, it seems impossible that any such thing, even approximately analagous, could take place in our time. Yet I should like to present, briefly, two recent examples (from, in fact, many, many) of simple information that was never really "secret," in the sense of being unavailable or inaccessible, but that did not come easily to our attention. Both of these items concern the much-reported, investigated, and studied war in Vietnam.

In the early spring of 1989, CBS reporter Morley Safer did a piece for the magazine-format news show "Sixty Minutes." Much of this he later incorporated into a book. He went to Vietnam and interviewed veterans of the other side, both North Vietnamese regulars and Vietcong guerillas, both high ranking and other ranks, to see how they "felt" about things. Not in response to any questions from Safer (and, indeed, he neither reacted to their statements on this matter nor asked any follow-up questions), each of these veterans announced that the bleakest and blackest time for him and his cause had been the Tet Offensive of 1968. During which, they all allowed, they had suffered something in excess of 50,000 men killed in action and had come urgently close to losing the whole war. This figure is, roughly, five times the number of enemy casualties claimed in any of the accounts of that battle that I know of, in books, television reports, newspaper and magazine pieces, etc. And all the American versions and histories, early and late, seem in complete agreement that the Tet Offensive was an American defeat and the turning point of the war against us. In part this negative view of the battle admitted the possibility that the military results had been favorable, but that the *perception,* enforced and reinforced by the American media, was of a disaster. .

Incidentally, General Giap, the North Vietnamese military commander during the war, gave their own number of dead as, roughly, 1,000,000. Which is very close to the ratio to population of our own Union dead.

A second major piece of surprising information concerning the war in Vietnam also delayed its appearance until the spring of 1989. On 16 May 1989, a Reuters story out of Hong Kong published in the *Washington Post* and elsewhere reported that the "semi-official" China News Service had for the first time stated some of the facts of China's direct involvement in the war in Vietnam. The Chinese admitted to giving more than twenty billion dollars in military aid to North Vietnam during the war. They also announced that they had sent 320,000 combat troops to fight against the Americans in Vietnam! (The peak of American involvement was, roughly, 500,000 men at one time.) Further, in passing, the Chinese mentioned that Soviet combat forces manned many of the North Vietnamese antiaircraft facilities and shot down American aircraft.

Yet another example of contemporary secrecy, this one planned by a nation-state and depending mainly (and, as it turns out, unsuccessfully) on ignorance and the failure of memory, found itself as a back-page story in the *New York*

Times for 24 March 1989: "At Buchenwald Now, No Mention of Jews." The *Times* article describes the fact that East Germany's memorial for the dead at Buchenwald does not anywhere mention two salient truths about that concentration camp: (a) that most of the victims were Jews, and (b) that the camp was liberated by the American Fourth Armored Division, their timely arrival saving something like 20,000 lives. The struggle to keep the memory of the Holocaust alive is, in itself, evidence of the difficulty of preserving the hard facts of recent history.

It would seem extremely difficult to keep all these facts and others secret and largely unknown to the exceedingly well-informed American public. But somehow it was so managed, and so it should be no large surprise that events occurring a hundred and more years ago in our history could be misconstrued and misunderstood.

There are other good reasons for our imaginative ignorance of the Civil War. First, the experience of the veterans of the Civil War was, by dint of the duration and the ferocity of the combat, finally, ineffable, incommunicable to those who had not shared the experience, except perhaps in the somewhat vague and abstract images of, say, Holmes's great valedictory speech. The veterans had passed beyond the possibility of communicable specificity. It then took many changes in the American literary language in our twentieth century for us to begin to create an uncoded language that can apprehend and report the particular truths of the Civil War.

(It is purest irony that we are at last capable of dealing with the past even as the codes of our own time, particularly the sociopolitical connotations and cryptograms of our codes, render us unable even to discuss or debate many clear and present dangers and burning issues.)

Secondly, the Civil War veterans had clearly passed beyond any hope or desire to use the peace that followed for anything else but healing. It is truly remarkable, if not unique in a historical sense, that nobody of any importance among the defeated even briefly contemplated the notion of returning to the battlefield later to try to settle many of the still-unsettled issues or even to restore the status quo. Very few wars have ended so completely and so coterminously with the conclusion of the official military action.

Third, when the war had ended, even the most outspoken of the military leaders on both sides saw it as their duty to bind up the nation's wounds and accept the consequences of both victory and defeat. You will remember, of course, Nathan Bedford Forrest's admonitions and injunctions to his soldiers in his farewell orders: "Civil War, such as you have just passed through, naturally engenders feelings of animosity, hatred and revenge. It is our duty to divest ourselves of all such feelings, and, so far as it is in our own power to do so, to cultivate feelings towards those with whom we have so long contested and heretofore so widely but honestly differed." At the end he put it all with a beautiful simplicity. Remember that this is a final military *order:* "You have been good soldiers, you can be good citizens. Obey the laws, preserve your honor, and the government to which you have surrendered can afford to be and will be magnanimous."

Yet another factor bringing the family, the great White Tribe, back together in a sense of honorable reunion, if not full reconciliation, was the hard-earned respect they had for each other as soldiers, as fighters. As Holmes put it in that same Memorial Day speech: "You could not stand up day after day, in those indecisive contests where overwhelming victory was impossible because neither side would run as they ought to when beaten, without getting at least something of the same brotherhood for the enemy that the north pole of a magnet has for the south, each working in an opposite sense to the other, but unable to get along without the other." Which is to say, among other things, that the blood and bones of *both sides* were necessary to and contributed to the one undeniable result of the war—the end of slavery.

Freedom for the slaves was purchased chiefly by the White Tribe, with more blood, rivers of it, offered up than for any other cause or enterprise I know of. I can find no other ready example out of all history of a majority tribe all but destroying itself on behalf of any minority group for any reason whatsoever. In all earlier and later judgments (some of them justly harsh) against the White Tribe, that must and deserves to be honorably remembered. If either or both sides had ever followed the logical dictates of reason, and not the imperatives of a passionate morality, there would certainly have been a compromise. Those who say that war changes nothing and accomplishes nothing must, at least, bear this huge exception in mind.

And, reason or not, if the North and South had not fought so well and so savagely and so long against each other, there would surely, likewise, have been a compromise. So it is that, indirectly at least, the dead Confederate soldiers have as much to do with the emancipation they resisted as the Northerners who imposed it.

Something else the changing White Tribe is entitled to remember, and not without honor and pride, is that the very ideals over which they fought each other to the death and against which they measured themselves and are even now, to this day, judged and measured against, the selfsame ideas and ideals that have come to be called "human rights," with all of the concomitant notions of personal freedom and justice and equity, these ideals came directly out of this tribe's history, its highest aspirations. If the Tribe, fairly judged by its own standards, has all too often failed to meet with and to live up to its own best hopes, it nevertheless holds the burden and the honor of introducing those hopes and ideals into the world's social and political dialogue, and finally, too, into the hearts and minds of all the tribes on this planet.

Be that as it may, we were, as a nation, a house divided, under two flags. And then we were one nation again.

4.

Whatever happened in that old house in Georgia?

The captain, according to his private plan, collected from friends and family at home all the latest magazines and fashion-pattern and sewing books being newly published in the peaceful and prosperous North. These things he left around the house, here and there, in odd places. And these things were studiously ignored whenever he was in the house. But they were studied and well thumbed whenever he was safely absent.

Thus all that was needed was for him to pretend, successfully, to be absent. And then to discover his covey of young women, sprawled on the window seats or on the rugs, whispering and giggling and poring over the Yankee magazines. Of course they responded to the discovery with fury. But fury, verbal fury, is an honest response. And it all ended in laughter rather than tears. And then, as the story is told and is believed, it ended in a marriage. Perhaps because, as our somewhat inhibited ancestors well knew, a woman's open and unadorned fury can be quite as naked and intimate a form of revelation as any other. That true love should follow behind its exposure is not altogether surprising.

It happened then and there in Georgia and then elsewhere in the family, and in the White Tribe, all across the South.

And in the time of resurrection and re-creation many old class lines and social fences broke down. When all are equally poor together, it is (as readers of Faulkner will have noticed) somewhat ridiculous to depend upon a social hierarchy based not on old money but on lost money. Truth is, money doesn't and can't count for much when there isn't any. For a long time, for as long as the South was, by any and all measures, essentially poor, that is from the Civil War until World War II and even after, there was a form of meritocracy, inequitable as all such hierarchies are, but, anyway, based more on service and accomplishment than on either inheritance or accumulation.

And so there were the two flags of peacetime, both seeming now to be as quaintly archaic as heraldic devices, here in our American world where the satisfaction of every kind of greed is so often dignified by being described as energetic achievement; where the only aristocracy seems to be celebrity, which itself is an accolade bestowed as willingly upon the criminal as the saint; a world that accords the same kind of weird and wicked equality upon Mother Teresa and Ted Bundy.

In my own family the division was between my mother's family and my father's. In a moment we shall return, as we soon and surely must, to the sidewalk in front of the drugstore in Kissimmee, Florida. Ideally, with much more time and space to play with and to play in I should now be able to present a lively and specific sketch of my mother's large family—for lively and charming people they were and they are, fun to be with and fun to remember and to talk about. Think of them as being blithe and flamboyant, attractive, widely and sometimes wildly gifted; there were and are still painters, musicians, dancers, and writers among them. Think of them, one and all, as easy come, easy go, in and out of the money, spending it rather than losing it, finally indifferent to it, generous to a fault, yet likewise shameless when in real or perceived need. Think of them as principled and honorable, but likewise tactful and reasonable in most matters. Except in whatever they took and take to be matters of personal honor. With that as a kind of hint or clue, go just a little deeper and picture them as angular and hard-edged, courageous often beyond the point of rashness (they will take any dare, answer any challenge). Also consistently violent. Joyously so, loving the plucked chords, the steel-thin country music and the stomping clog dance of aroused adrenaline. Picture them, then and now, as riddled with casualties, ravaged by self-destruction. Picture them as good friends and good company, as easy to like (sometimes to love) as to envy. And impossible to admire very much.

Their finest hours have always been in the wars. They have fought in all the wars. And their finest war was the Civil War. For which it would seem they were programmed. Under two inner flags themselves, part Hotspur and part Falstaff (with also maybe a little touch of Ancient Pistol in the night), they are and always have been, except for during that one bloody era, somewhat out of time and out-of-date.

My father and his clan were and are out-of-date also. But in a different way. Think of them as hard to like but almost impossible not to admire. And ask their enemies. Think of them as impossible not to fear.

5.

At the time we were talking about, that evening in front of the drugstore, my father and his law partner were actively fighting against the Ku Klux Klan. The Klan was a real political power in central Florida, as elsewhere, in those days. Not a sad little bunch of poor Fundamentalists and ignorant rednecks and racists in bedsheets, but a real clan, a down-home, native-grown kind of organized crime family. My father and his partner were fighting against the Klan in public and in the courthouses with the promise that they would, as they did, serve and represent and defend free of charge any person at all who chose to resist the Klan and felt the need of a lawyer.

This exposed position soon led to a whole lot of trouble, believe me. And it also led, after a time, to the demise of the Klan as any kind of a political power in Florida. And not those events alone, but also the purpose and character of my father, led him (with the rest of us tagging along) to an odd kind of power of his own, based on fear and respect in equal measure in courtrooms all the way from Pensacola and Tallahassee to Miami (and, yes, several times in the chamber of the Supreme Court of the United States). He became, before the end of his life, a maker and breaker of politicians and of corporations, a man who gave much of his time, and thus a very large part of his real and potential earnings (thus, also, of my inheritance) to the service of the poor, the oppressed, the ignored and downtrodden. He was a man of no common vices at all and of very few flaws of character except for a very violent temper, a casual indifference to many of the habits and customs of diplomatic good manners and social tact, and a certain kind of earned pride that was unbending and unbreakable. He lived with and by an austerity that would have challenged the courage and dedication and self-discipline of a Ralph Nader, though he never sought to impose his personal self-discipline upon others, even our own family, except by example. Open and generous, he did not seem especially to admire the austerity of others, at least for its own sake, finding it to be, as it so often is, a kind of inverted hypocrisy.

When he died, his great and surprising tribute was in the swarm of the poor, both black and white, who came by the anonymous hundreds, a huge crowd of common people, fanning and fisting like a flock of swallows or swifts in a wide, windy sky.

Rebellious then, as now, I spurned that inheritance and have walked in my own and different ways under two flags, though I often find myself ghosted and haunted by his example. I find that I truly believe that anyone who will not risk and sacrifice everything for his or her principles is, in truth, unprincipled. And I discover in myself a strong and deep feeling that virtuous acts that lead to any kind of profit or reward or, as I have come to believe, to any forms of conventional honor and respect, are not so much beneath contempt as unworthy of serious attention.

And I am astonished to have to admit that much as I love the lively arts, including the art of letters, to which so much of my life has been dedicated, I cannot accept that a life based mainly upon aesthetic principles can be anything but harmlessly silly at best and, in view of all this world's desperate needs and hungers, shameful at worst.

I know that is his voice speaking to me, in all those things, though I also know I may be guilty of mistranslating him.

But all of this came later on. This simple little story took place early. And just as the lines of battle were being drawn and the fight was getting under way.

6.

There we all were, trooping outside to look at the taillights. They didn't work, all right, because they were broken, and there was shattered red glass in the street right behind the back bumper.

"I wonder who would do a thing like that," my father said, giving the young cop a hard look.

"Well, I wouldn't know, sir," he said. "I just work for the city and I do what I'm told. And now I have to write you a ticket."

"Fine," my father said. "I understand that."

Then he surprised the cop and us too by asking if he could pay for the ticket right then and there. And the cop said yes, that was his legal right, and he said it would cost five dollars.

Now that was considerable money in those days, when grown men with skills were earning eight or ten dollars a week. Nobody had any money in those days, nobody we knew or knew of. Most of my father's clients, those who could pay at all, paid him in produce and fresh eggs, things like that.

My father peeled off five one-dollar bills. The cop wrote him a receipt. Then my father told my mother to drive us on home when we had finished our ice cream. He had to go somewhere.

He whistled loudly and waved his good arm. A taxi came right over from the Atlantic Coastline depot directly across the way. He kissed my mother on the cheek and said he would be back just as soon as he could. Gave her the keys to our car and hopped into the cab.

None of us heard what he told the driver: "Let's go to Tallahassee."

Tallahassee was and is the state capital, a good three hundred and more miles away. By bad, narrow roads in those days.

Much later we learned what happened. They arrived very late. Slept in the cab. First thing in the morning my father got himself a shave in the barbershop. Then went to the legislature. Where, exercising a constitutional right to speak on this kind of matter, he quickly established that the town charter for Kissimmee, Florida, was completely illegal and unconstitutional. In a technical, legal sense that town did not exist and never had. It would require a special action of the state legislature to give the town a new charter and a legal existence. Having made his point, he thanked the legislators kindly for their time and left the Capitol. Woke the snoring taxi driver and said: "Let's go back home."

It probably cost him a hundred dollars for that ride. Maybe more. He never told us, and nobody, not even my mother, ever dared to ask him.

By the time he arrived home there was a delegation waiting to see him at our house—the mayor, the chief of police, the judge, pretty much the whole gang. Legislators had been on the phone all day to them, and they were deeply worried. Because, you see, everything they had ever done, in the absence of a valid town charter, including collecting taxes, had been completely illegal.

"What do you want from us, Garrett?"

"I knew it would come down to that. And I'm glad it did, because as it happens there is something I do want from you all."

They were all looking and waiting. I reckon they were ready to do or pay most anything.

"Damn you!" he said. "I want my five dollars back from that phony traffic ticket."

Long pause.

"That's all?"

"That's all. You give me my five dollars back and I'll give you back your receipt."

So they paid him the five dollars and he tore the receipt in two and they filed politely out of the house.

"Well, you beat them," I said. "You won!"

"That's right, boy," he told me. "And I taught them a very important lesson."

"What's that?" my mother asked nervously.

"If they want to stop me now," he said, "they're going to have to kill me. And I don't think they've got the guts for it."

Then he laughed out loud. And so did I, not because it was so funny, but because it seemed like the right thing to do at the time.

The Gift:
A Recapitulation

You know how the grandfather died. Died not badly. If, by that, by *badly,* you mean dying after a long, slow, painful, and probably inordinately expensive illness. Was more than ninety years old, still able if somewhat fragile, able to move about and to look after himself, still alert and thoughtful and blessed and cursed by a clear memory, though he sometimes complained, saying that he remembered or dreamed things he would rather not have. Died quietly, dreaming or dreamless in deep sleep in his own bed and his own house after only a few days of not feeling so very well. Feeling a little poorly, thank you.

Died not badly or poorly, though he did sure enough die poor. Not as poor as you can be and still be alive, that's true. God knows, and so do we, that we bear witness to enough of that in fact and flesh and in the flickering images on our TV screens. He had his social security and a few dollars above and beyond that thanks to some of his working children and grandchildren. Lived those last years, after busy years spent elsewhere, in a raw and simple frame house, a sturdy one-story shack, really, set up on stilts because it was built on a little spit of land close by tidal water. Certain winds and tides would sometimes get together and let the rising water come to lap against the front steps. He said at times it was like being on a boat again.

Lived not all alone, but with always a couple of hound dogs (who, like the animals out of the old stories and myths, crawled up under the house and cried and howled for three days after he died.) Always dogs and cats and some chickens and once upon a time a pet turkey gobbler and, oh yes, a country woman, lean and pale and younger by many years, a cracker woman if the truth is known and said out loud. (Which was and is seldom if ever.) A lean, pale, more than a little careless and slovenly cracker woman who could cook the plain Southern food that suited him, and also kept his house for him, more or less, as clean as she knew how to. A companion, then. Some kind of a distant cousin and blood kin to him and to all the rest of us. Though that truth was seldom, if ever, alluded to, either. And when it unavoidably was mentioned, it was all vague enough, the women, keepers of family and Tribal flame and memories, being uniformly unspecific as to how close and what kind of kin to us that woman might be. When he died in his sleep and the dogs crept underneath and took to howling, she, too, slipped away (with no tears anybody heard or saw) and with most of the family flat silver and whatever modest valuables were handy and portable. Though who could blame her for taking anything she could carry with her? And, anyway, she didn't take it all, not even very much of it, did she? There were things left over, some of them precious only by memory and association, true, for everyone in the family to have and to share, after all.

You yourself have his best gold pocket watch and watch chain, don't you? Must remember to take it to a jeweler and have it cleaned and set one of these days.

But this is not a story about that. Not exactly. Maybe not at all. We'll see. This story goes back years and years before that. Before you were born and able to see and feel and think for yourself. You were a witness only to the last part, that part you have already told. And you probably told it first, started there to try to identify and perhaps prove yourself at the outset as a kind of credible witness. Someone at least entitled to imagine and to believe in the time before your time.

This story begins by going back to the time when, for a time, he was a rich man of good repute. A man with an earned reputation as a man of honor and industry and dignity and integrity and courage and style and so forth and so on. All of those things that facts of wealth and good fortune, in and of themselves, could not and cannot confer outright upon anyone. But nevertheless there are, as we well know, qualities that wealth and good fortune can greatly enhance and help to maintain and preserve. Whereas the chief qualities of character and repute that can conceivably arise out of conditions of poverty and bad luck are apt to be more inward and spiritual than outward and visible. Way of the world.

Old father Job has some words of wisdom on that subject. But this is not a story as bleakly sad as his. Nor does ours come, as you already know, to a happy ending.

Our man made two great fortunes in his lifetime and he spent three. Which is how they always politely described it. He made his money honestly and honorably enough, according to the lights and mores of those times. (Which, may I say, were in many ways and means more strict than our own hypocritical guidelines.) Made it not by stealing anything from

anyone. Not by any kind of clever gouging or any sharp prac-
tices. Not by cruelty and arrogant indifference to the needs
of others. Not by tricks of the trade.

Hard to believe or imagine such things nowadays, isn't
it? In part you choose to credit it to the circumstances of the
times. A time when good name seemed to matter so very
much, maybe most of all. Therefore a time when shame was
still possible. Call it all a kind of hypocrisy, if you choose to,
but bear in mind how many of our own hypocrisies are the
forces that lead us, ready and willing or not, to try to act
virtuously.

In some ways the whole story is so aptly familiar to its
times, so shaped like a work of fiction, that it may challenge
credulity. Consider the orphan child raised by poor kinfolk
and coming to manhood and maturity in the long, shadowy
days of the Reconstruction South. Growing up, as it happened, only a few hundred yards away from and in the same
village as the place he returned to and died in. From early
childhood having learned to be perfectly at home in deep
woods and on the open water. His first work for a living,
while still no more than a large child, involved both sea and
forest. Cutting timber and bringing it out with mules. Then
with an old man in charge, sailing boatloads of timber down
the coast and into the Charleston harbor. Where once, when
he was still very young, not yet twelve years old, the old man
was knocked unconscious by the boom and the boy had to
bring in the large clumsy schooner, through wind and rough
water, all by himself. As soon as he was old enough he was
licensed as a pilot. Then earned and saved and with those
earnings and savings studied and learned the law. Then practiced law, soon with success and later on with honor and high
offices. Married a beautiful and gifted woman and with her
had and raised his family of five sons and three daughters.

And you have seen them for yourself in old and slowly fading photographs, all standing solemnly, straight-facedly together. Except, sometimes, for a white-haired great-grandmother sitting on an incongruous chair in the midst of them. Live oaks set the scene like columns. Leafy, mossy canopies all around them, casting a wealth of light and shadow. And themselves standing together a little stiffly, darkly handsome and somehow enigmatic as they squint to stare out of that dappled shade and across time as if from some other, far shore, all attention fixed on an unseen and now-unknown photographer.

It is another side of that life and times, his, that has always interested you most. You were a child, then a young man, and loved to hear anything and everything about his passion rooted in the cold indifference of the archetypal gambler. Gambling meant not merely with money and possessions, which he surely did, but, in his daily courtroom trade, for instance, with life and death. Betting it all on life and love and light as you yourself wrote about it in a poem a long time ago.

Lucky and at the very peak of his good luck and wordly wisdom, he had a whole and enviable stable of horses—trotters and pacers and jumpers and fine carriage horses and riding horses and ponies for the children. And automobiles, too, when they began to arrive and to be part of the scene. Because his sons, your uncles, rose early to take the cars before he could or was ready to, he had six automobiles, finally, scattered all around the yard. They were living in those days in Ortega, across the wide Saint John's River from Jacksonville. And, so the story goes, one morning he took his car, last of the six remaining when he finished breakfast, and drove it to town to work. Stalled on the narrow drawbridge at its high center. Couldn't start that car if his life depended on it.

Struggled with the obstinate machine while all behind him a restless line, a mob of other cars and horse-drawn carriages, and probably the crowded streetcar, too, honked and hooted and tooted, jeered and hollered. Then he, weary of all that, climbing out of his car, stepping lightly off the high running board and walking to the edge of the bridge and dropping the car keys over the rail, seeing them glint and glitter in the light and flash, white and brief as a gull's wing, as they hit and splashed and sank to the deep bottom. Looked down and saw the keys vanishing forever, then walked away to his office, to work, never looking back and (as they all said ever after) never once asking about and never once caring what became of that stalled automobile.

What a time he had!

Hunted big game in far places—Africa and India and the Arctic. And when the family enjoyed an inland vacation, in the mountains of western North Carolina or maybe in the villages and old farms of Vermont, why, it took a whole railroad car to carry them and their companions and servants there and back. By sea he had the use of his own steam yacht, the *Cosette,* lean and fast at ninety feet and drawing so little water that he could nose her into many a small harbor, shallow river, or creek. In the open sea, the Atlantic, he, himself, handled her in good weather and foul. For the fun of it sometimes challenged other yachts to race. None ever came close to beating the *Cosette.*

All of that and almost everything else except for odds and ends, flotsam and jetsam of his life, was long gone before you were born. Gone, too, now that you suddenly think about it, gone by the time he was your age.

Anyway, all of this interests you, fascinates with an odd kind of feeling, as you grow old with your few and perfectly commonplace possessions, owning nothing at all you would fear to shed, nothing you cheerfully couldn't do without. Nothing you have is worth more than a shrug, really. Except for memories. Which, of course, have to include his life and the lives of others.

Remembering now, at least for here and now, one moment among them all.

He would have been middle-aged then. Getting on, as they used to say. All of his children grown up and gone away except for the two youngest—Jack and Chester. Jack who would soon become a fine professional golfer and later a drunkard. Chester, the dancer, soon to dance in great cities all over the world. And then soon after that to fight in the Second World War and live to see it end at Linz, meeting the Russians on the bridge over the Danube there. There in Linz where, by the mysterious and wonderful synchronicity of things, you were to find yourself on duty, sometimes on guard duty at a checkpoint on the selfsame bridge.

But then, on that day, in those days, they were boys still. The last of his boys. And it was, happened to be, the birthday of one or the other of them. I forget which. And does it matter? Not worth mentioning or worrying about now, really, except insofar as it gives an apt occasion and an edge of anticipation to the playing out of the story. At least from their point of view. For, in a sense, it's their story more than his, even though it is about him.

As they would learn gradually and later, it was on this very same day, and all day long, that he gambled grandly and lost his last fortune. Last of it. All of it. Everything he owned in the world. Except for the house in Ortega, which he would soon enough have to sell just to make ends meet. In one bad day he had managed to lose everything except the cash he had in his wallet. Two hundred dollars. Which was no small sum by any standard or measure in those days. Ten or twenty times what it would be equal to today.

They had come over to town in one of the cars to pick him up at the office and to bring him home for the birthday dinner. He came out of the front door of the office building at a minute or two past five, neat as a pin in his three-piece suit, his tailored shirt and tie. From high white separate collar to the fold of his cuffs, as neat and crisp, unwilted and unwrinkled as he had looked in the morning when he left for work. That was his style and was not even noticed by them until much later, when they tried together to reconstruct that day he had lived through, spent—even as all his little house of cards collapsed and fell apart and was shuffled, and then he was dealt out a sequence of impossible and implausible hands to play and to lose with. He came out of the entrance to the building, most likely nodding a good evening to the doorman, crossed the sidewalk, smiling a greeting to them where they sat in the car, parked with the motor running, at the curb.

"It's a lovely day," he said, looking up and around at blue skies, thin clouds, light breeze. "And I've been cooped up in my office all day long. Let's leave the car and walk home."

A walk of several miles. But it was a fine day. And why not? He gave the doorman the keys to the car and a coin or two. They set off walking in the direction of the Saint John's River.

Closer to the water, they came across a hand-lettered sign pointing down a narrow lane to a dock. Advertising a boat for sale. They paused a moment, went to take a look.

It was a fat little wooden sailboat, single mast, cockpit, high railed. A native version, squat and sturdy, of a New

England catboat. Only a little bit larger. Looked in pretty good shape, all in all, though no doubt she could use some paint on her bottom. The man who owned her and was selling her came out of an unpainted shed nearby. Fellow with rubber boots and a beard flecked with gray and a grin with raggedy teeth.

And then their father, your grandfather, took off his coat, loosened his necktie, and hunkered down with the old fellow to bargain for the boat. A duet of mumbling and of pauses. More muttering and silence. Old-timer stood up and hawked and spit a gob over the edge of the dock into the lapping water.

Your grandfather stands up, too, and shakes his legs lightly to let his trousers fall neatly into place.

"Done, then," he says.

Offers his hand and shakes on it. Then pulls out his wallet and counts off a hundred dollars to pay the old man.

"It's yours," he says to the boys, or to whichever one was having the birthday nobody can remember now. "Let's sail home. Plenty of time left before the light starts to fade, and"— here looking out at wrinkles of wind sprinting across the river, at the wind and the glitter of small waves—"it's a nice breeze."

They sit down side by side on the dock and untie and remove their street shoes and socks. Barefoot they step on board and stow their shoes. Carefully stow his folded coat. Unfurl and check the sail. Fix the centerboard, rudder, and tiller in place. The old man returns and adds a paddle to the deal. They untie the ropes fore and aft, paddle a moment or two to clear the end of the dock. And then your grandfather settles into place and taxes up the tiller and the sheet. She luffs briefly, catches wind, and in a moment is pointed and skimming, heeling slightly, on a starboard tack.

It's going to take them an hour or so, not a lot more, taking turns at the tiller, to bring her home to their own dock and float at their house. When they do get there, the wind will be up and shifting direction and the tide will be turning. And it will be a little tricky to come in and dock her gracefully. The boys will ask him to do it himself, half-hoping, it may well be, that he has lost his touch and will bang and shake them all when he rams the float. Unspoken, it's a kind of a bet or a dare. And, of course, he takes the dare. A kind of a last bet (as he has always bet on life and love and light) with half of all his remaining wealth in the world. Betting nothing at all, and yet, for a moment, everything that matters. He takes hold of the tiller and sheet, swings around, and runs with the wind as if to crash into the float. Boys are holding tight now and gritting their teeth when he suddenly yanks the tiller toward him and jibes her. She swings around and he lets the sheet loose and the sail crackles and luffs as, urged on by her own slight wake, she lightly touches the float. They leap out and snub and tie her fast. Remove the mast and furl the sail. Pull up the rudder and raise the centerboard and then sit side by side to put on their shoes. Sun going down, wind touched with a chill and the salty sense of the open sea.

"Nice little boat," he tells them. "A little clumsy, but she'll get you there."

They tote all the things, including the paddle. While he walks in the middle between them, his arms over their shoulders as they go along up the twisty path from the riverbank towards the shape of the house among the trees, house where, window by window, evening lights are coming on.

"You know," one of those brothers, your uncles, will tell you so many years later, "I don't think I ever saw Papa as happy as that. Sailing that boat home with not a worry in the world."

That's how he sees it and remembers it. How he takes it to be.

Well, why not? This is not the story of Job. Nothing like that. Only another story of winning and losing. Lightened by a gesture, the last real gift. Anyway, the children of fortune seldom arrive at happy endings.

Of course, it's not the same for you at second hand. You can't and won't come to believe that the inevitable shabby end of things would not lie heavy upon even the stoutest of hearts. But, still, consider that he seems to have known a blithe and simple way to lift his flagging spirits. First by an impulse and an act of unthinking generosity. And next by giving himself over to it—to water and air, to the fire of fading sunlight on the river, and to the solid earth of a smooth landing and a safe return. And thereby all the rest of it, beginning and end, bitter or sweet, is nothing at all. Good luck and bad luck, all the rest of it, none of it means or matters anything at all.